THE INFAMOUS ITALIAN'S SECRET BABY

BY
CAROLE MORTIMER

MILLS & BOON®

First published in Great Britain 2009
Harlequin Mills & Boon Limited,
Eton House, 18-24 Paradise Road, Richmond, Surrey TW9 1SR

© Carole Mortimer 2009

ISBN: 978 0 263 87445 7

Set in Times Roman 10½ on 12 pt
01-1109-44798

Harlequin Mills & Boon policy is to use papers that are natural, renewable and recyclable products and made from wood grown in sustainable forests. The logging and manufacturing process conform to the legal environmental regulations of the country of origin.

Printed and bound in Spain
by Litografia Rosés, S.A., Barcelona

THE INFAMOUS ITALIAN'S SECRET BABY

PROLOGUE

'THE party is outside by the pool.'

Bella froze in the doorway, searching the shadows of the unlit room she had entered by mistake, a study or den if the book-lined walls and desk were any indication. Her hand tightened about the door-handle as she finally saw the outline of the large, imposing figure seated behind that desk.

The man was totally unmoving, and yet his very stillness was an implied danger, an echo of the challenge in his tone. By the light from the hallway behind her, Bella was just able to make out the fall of long dark hair that grew onto a pair of wide shoulders, those shoulders and a powerful chest encased in a dark top of some kind.

She swallowed hard before speaking. 'I was looking for the bathroom…'

'As you can see, this is not it,' he responded, his amused voice slightly accented. As he spoke some of the tension left his upper torso and he relaxed back in the high-backed chair, head tilted slightly sideways as the glitter of his gaze moved slowly over Bella standing silhouetted in the doorway. 'Or perhaps you cannot see…'

Bella barely had time to realise that the husky voice sounded vaguely familiar before there was the click of a switch and a light illuminated the desk in a soft warm glow. And the man seated behind it. Bella recognised him instantly.

Gabriel Danti!

Bella felt her heart plummet in her chest as she looked at the wickedly handsome man in front of her. His thick dark hair and chocolate-brown eyes were almost black in their intensity. His olive-skinned face boasted a perfectly straight aristocratic nose, high cheekbones, a mouth that was full and sensual, and a square, arrogant chin, softened only by the slight cleft in its centre.

It was the face that thousands, no, *millions* of women all over the world sighed over. Daydreamed over. Drooled over!

Italian by birth, Gabriel Danti was, at the age of twenty-eight, the defending champion of the Formula One racing car championship currently in its fifth month. This man was the darling of the rich and the famous on both sides of the Atlantic—and, as if that weren't enough, he was also the only son and heir of Cristo Danti, head of the Danti business and wine empire, with vineyards in both Italy and America.

Even while she registered all those things about him Bella was also aware of the fact that this house in the Surrey countryside was Gabriel Danti's English home, and that he was actually the host of the noisy party taking place outside by the pool. So what was he doing sitting up here alone in the dark?

She moistened suddenly dry lips. 'I'm terribly sorry for disturbing you. I really *was* looking for the bathroom.' She gave a small self-conscious grimace. How awful that the first and probably only time she had the opportunity to speak to Gabriel Danti it was because she needed to find the bathroom!

Gabriel made a lazy study of the tiny, dark-haired woman who stood in the doorway of his study. A young woman totally unlike the tall, leggy blondes that he usually escorted—and totally unlike the traitorous Janine, he acknowledged grimly to himself.

She had very long, straight hair, as black as ebony and falling soft and silky about her shoulders. A dark fringe of that same silky softness lay on her forehead, and her small, heart-shaped face was pale and smooth as alabaster—and totally dominated by a pair of the most unusual violet-coloured eyes Gabriel had ever seen. Her gently pouting lips were unknowingly sensuous and inviting.

His gaze dropped lower, to the soft woollen top she wore, which was the same violet colour of her eyes. The top two buttons were undone to reveal surprisingly full breasts—completely naked breasts beneath the thinness of her sweater, if Gabriel wasn't mistaken, which made her slender waist look even more so in comparison. Her narrow hips and legs were clearly defined in figure-hugging jeans.

That long, leisurely glance told Gabriel that he didn't know her.

But he wanted to!

Bella took an involuntary step back as Gabriel Danti stood up from behind the desk, revealing that the top he wore was in fact a black silk shirt that rippled as he stood before resettling softly against the muscled hardness of his shoulders and chest. The sleeves were turned back to just below his elbows, revealing muscled forearms lightly dusted with dark hair.

At least a foot taller than her own five feet two inches, Gabriel Danti at once dominated the space around him. And she, Bella realised in some alarm as she found herself rooted to the spot, was totally unable to move as the tall Italian sauntered across the room in long feline strides to stand mere inches in front of her. The raucous noise of the party outside instantly became muted as all Bella could see or hear was him.

She had been wrong, Bella mused as she found herself in a daze, unable to look away from the dark beauty of his face. Gabriel Danti wasn't handsome. He was stunningly gorgeous.

Bella could feel the heat radiating from his body, could smell his tangy aftershave, the male scent of him that invaded and claimed the senses, filling her with a warm lethargy, a need to move closer to all that heady maleness.

A need Bella was unable to resist as she felt herself swaying towards him. She made an effort at the last moment not to do so, lifting a hand to stop herself from curving her body along the length of his. Instead she found the palm of her hand against the black silk of his shirt, her fingers curling against the warm hardness of the chest beneath as she felt the hot, heady thrum of his heart against her fingertips.

What was happening to her?

She never reacted to men like this. At least, she never had before…

She had to—

Bella froze, every part of her immobilised as Gabriel Danti raised one of his long elegant hands that so capably handled the wheel of a racing car travelling at unimaginable speeds, and cupped her chin, the soft pad of his thumb caressing lightly across her bottom lip. The tingling warmth that ensued travelled down her throat and spine to pool hotly between her thighs.

Dark brown eyes held her own captive. 'You have the most beautiful eyes I have ever seen.' His voice was low, husky, as if he were aware that anything else would break the spell that surrounded them.

'So do you,' Bella breathed, her chest rising and falling sharply with the effort it took to breathe at all.

His throaty laugh was a soft rumble beneath her fingertips before it faded; the darkness of his gaze suddenly became intense, searching. 'Did you come here with someone?'

Bella blinked, trying to think through the slow insidiousness of his seduction. 'I—I'm here with a group of friends, Mr Danti.' She gave a self-conscious shake of her head as his eyes compelled her answer. 'Sean is the nephew of one of your mechanics.'

It didn't surprise Gabriel that this beautiful young woman knew who he was. Even if she hadn't recognised him from the photographs of him that appeared almost daily in the newspapers at the moment, the fact that this was his house and he had been sitting in the study where several framed photographs of him winning races also adorned the walls would have given him away.

'Sean is your boyfriend?' There was a slight edge to his voice that hadn't been there seconds earlier.

'Heavens, no!' she denied with a smile, her long hair falling forward across her breasts as she shook her head. 'We're just at university together. I hope you don't mind that Sean brought some friends with him, Mr Danti?' She was frowning now, her eyes almost purple. 'His uncle said—'

'I do not mind,' Gabriel cut in reassuringly. 'And please call me Gabriel.'

A slight flush darkened her cheeks. 'And I'm Bella,' she invited huskily.

'Bella?'

'Isabella.' She grimaced. 'But everyone just calls me Bella.'

Gabriel wasn't sure he wanted to be grouped with 'everyone' where this fascinating woman was concerned. He raised one dark brow. 'You are Italian?'

'No,' she laughed softly, her teeth small and white against the fullness of her lips. 'My mother allowed my father, who's a doctor, to choose my own and my younger sister's names, so he named us after two of his favourite models and actresses: Isabella and Claudia. When my brother was born six years ago my mother had the choice of names. She chose Liam. After the actor. A tall Irishman, with what my mother describes as "very sexy blue eyes"—'

'I know him,' Gabriel admitted.

'You know of him or you know him?' Bella was aware that she was talking too much. About things that could be of absolutely no interest to a man like Gabriel Danti. It was nerves, that was what it was. That and the fact that she couldn't think straight with Gabriel's fingers still curled possessively around the softness of her chin!

The Italian smiled. 'I know him. I cannot confirm the sexiness of his blue eyes, of course, but—'

'You're mocking me now,' Bella reproved self-consciously.

'Only a little,' Gabriel murmured, his gaze once more intense on hers. 'You said you are at university?'

'Was,' Bella corrected ruefully. 'I left last month.'

Telling Gabriel that Bella was probably aged twenty-one or twenty-two to his twenty-eight. 'What subject did you study?'

'Art and History,' she supplied.

'With a view to teaching, perhaps?'

'I'm really not sure yet. I'm hoping something that involves both subjects.' She shrugged slender shoulders, the movement giving Gabriel, with his superior height, a delicious glimpse of the fullness of her breasts.

Gabriel could never remember being so instantly attracted to a woman before. So attracted that he was sure her appraisal of him earlier had raised his body temperature by several degrees, at the same time making him totally aware of every muscle and sinew of his own body as well as hers. Rousing a need, a hunger, inside him that demanded the slender curves of Bella's body be placed against his much harder ones. Intimately. Preferably with no clothing between them.

Bella gave a slightly nervous laugh as she saw the way the Italian's eyes had suddenly darkened. 'If you'll excuse me, I think I'll just go and find the bathroom—'

'The bathroom is the room next to this on the right,' Gabriel interrupted, his fingers firming against her chin. 'While you are gone, I suggest I find a bottle of champagne and some glasses and then we can find somewhere more comfortable in which to continue this conversation, hmm?'

What conversation? Bella wondered, slightly bemused. She was pretty sure that Gabriel Danti didn't want to hear more about her degree in art and history or her family! 'Shouldn't you be returning to your guests?' She frowned.

His laugh was slightly wicked. 'Does it sound as if they are missing me?'

Well…no, the party outside sounded noisier and more out of control than ever. Which was some feat considering several of the guests had already thrown off their clothes and jumped into the pool naked before Bella had left to go in search of the bathroom. Which had hastened her need to go in search of the bathroom, if she was honest; the party looked in danger of disintegrating in a way Bella wasn't at all comfortable with.

It had sounded like a fun thing to do when Sean Davies had invited several of his fellow ex-students to the party being given at the Surrey home of Gabriel Danti. A chance to mix with the rich and the famous.

The fact that most of those 'rich and famous' were behaving in a way Bella would never have imagined if she hadn't seen it with her own eyes had come as something of a shock to her. It wasn't that she was a prude, it was just a little disconcerting to have a man she had last seen reading the evening news, a respected middle-aged man, jumping stark naked into Gabriel Danti's swimming pool. Admittedly it was a warm summer's evening, but even so!

'Come, Bella.' Gabriel removed his hand from her chin only to place it about her waist, his arm warm and spine-tingling as it rested against the slenderness of her back. 'Do you have any preference in champagne?'

'Preference?' she echoed. Champagne was champagne, wasn't it?

'White or pink?' he elaborated.

'Er—pink will be fine.' As a student, the only preference Bella had when it came to wines was that it not cost a lot of money! 'Are you sure you wouldn't rather just rejoin your guests?' Bella hesitated in the hallway, rather confused that this gorgeous man, a man any of his female guests would scratch another woman's eyes out in order to spend time alone with, appeared to want to spend that time with *her*…

'I am very sure, Bella.' Gabriel turned her in the curve of his arm so that she now faced him, his hands resting lightly against her waist. 'But perhaps you would rather return to your friends…?'

Bella swallowed hard as Gabriel made no effort to hide the hot sensuality burning in his eyes. 'No, I—' She stopped as she realised her voice was several octaves higher than normal. She cleared her throat before trying again. 'No, I think I would enjoy drinking champagne with you more.'

Those dark eyes gleamed with satisfaction as he raised his hands to cup either side of her face before slowly lowering his head to take possession of her mouth. Sipping, tasting, his tongue was a warm sweep against her lips as he tacitly asked her permission to enter. Then he claimed her mouth, groaning low in his throat as Bella gave in to temptation, parting her lips and inviting his tongue to surge inside.

His mouth was hot against hers now, Bella feeling

slightly dizzy from the warm rush of desire that instantly claimed her. Her breasts were firm and aching and she moved instinctively to rub that ache against the hardness of Gabriel's chest, that friction affording her some relief even as she felt more desire pooling between her thighs.

Oh, how she wanted this man. Wanted him as she had never known it was possible to want any man, the hot demand of his kiss, the hardness of his thighs against hers, telling her that he returned that need.

Gabriel had never tasted anything as sweet as the response of Bella's mouth beneath his. Never felt anything so lush, so perfect, as his hands moved down over her hips and then down to clasp her bottom as he pulled her into him, his arousal now nestled demandingly against the flatness of her stomach.

Gabriel dragged his mouth from Bella's to cast a searching look down at her. Those beautiful violet-coloured eyes were so darkly purple it was almost impossible to distinguish the black of her pupils. Her cheeks were flushed, her lips swollen from their kisses, and she looked more erotically enticing than ever. Her breasts were firm against his chest, and Gabriel was able to feel the hardness of her nipples through the soft silk of his shirt.

'Go. Before I lose all sense and make love to you out here in the hallway!' He grasped the tops of her arms tightly and turned her in the direction of the bathroom she had been seeking. 'I will return in two minutes with the champagne and glasses.'

Bella was completely dazed and disorientated as she entered the bathroom and closed the door behind her before leaning weakly back against it.

She was twenty-one years of age, had dated dozens of boys in the last five or six years, but never before had she known anyone or anything as lethal—as potent—as Gabriel's kisses!

Bella straightened to look at herself in the mirror on the door of the bathroom cabinet over the sink. Her cheeks glowed with the warmth of her arousal. Her mouth—oh, dear, her lips were swollen and slightly parted as if in invitation! Her eyes were deep pools of liquid violet, the pupils enlarged. As for her breasts…Well, if she had any sense she would leave now! If she had any will power at all, she would *make* herself leave now.

Even as she told herself these things Bella knew she wasn't going anywhere but back into Gabriel Danti's arms…

'Nice?'

'Mmm.'

'Would you like more?'

'Please.'

'Come a little closer, then. Now hold out your hand.'

Bella lifted the hand holding her glass to allow Gabriel to pour her more champagne as she sat on the sofa beside him, at the same time noting that he hadn't touched any of the bubbly wine in his own glass since placing it on the coffee table in front of them. The two of them were seated in a sitting-room at the front of the house on the first floor, well away from the noisy party downstairs.

'You aren't drinking,' she pointed out in an effort to cover up the slight shaking of her hand as she once again raised her glass to her lips and took a sip of the delicious pink champagne.

He shook his head, his arm along the back of the sofa as he sat very close beside her, that hand playing with the silken strands of her hair. 'I'm going to the track for a practice session tomorrow, and I never drink if I am going to drive the next day.'

Bella's eyes widened. 'You shouldn't have bothered opening a bottle of champagne just for me.'

'It is not just for you,' Gabriel assured her, dipping his finger into her champagne glass before running his finger lightly behind Bella's ear and along her jaw. 'I said I do not drink champagne before driving, Bella, not that I do not intend enjoying its taste,' he murmured softly, his breath warm against her ear lobe as his lips moved to follow the trail of champagne left by his finger, his tongue rasping against her already sensitised skin.

The combination of Bella and champagne was more intoxicating to Gabriel's senses than drinking a whole bottle of the expensive wine could ever have been, her skin so smooth to the touch, its sweet taste driving the heat through Gabriel's already roused body until he throbbed with the need to touch her more intimately. All of her.

He held her gaze as he deliberately dipped his finger back into the champagne before leaving a moist trail from her chin, down the delicate curve of her throat, to the exposed swell of the fullness of her breasts, his lips instantly following that heady trail.

Bella squirmed pleasurably as the warmth of his mouth lingered on her breasts. 'Gabriel—'

'Let me, Bella,' he pressed huskily. 'Let me bathe you in champagne. All of you. So that I might drink from your body.' His hand moved to cup her cheek as his thumb moved across her parted lips once more. 'Will you allow me to do that, Bella?'

Bella had accepted exactly where this was going the moment she had agreed to accompany Gabriel up the stairs to what had turned out to be the private sitting-room that adjoined his bedroom. Although thankfully the bedroom door had remained closed, otherwise she might have panicked long before now.

Not that she was panicking. Quivering with delicious anticipation more described her present state of mind! Just the thought of Gabriel dribbling champagne over her totally naked body, before slowly licking away each drop with the rasp of his arousing tongue, was enough to heat every inch of her to a tingling awareness that suddenly made the few clothes Bella was wearing feel tight and restrictive.

'As long as I can reciprocate.' She dipped her own finger into the champagne before running that finger over the firm sensuality of Gabriel's slightly parted lips. 'May I?' She paused expectantly with her mouth only centimetres away from his, violet eyes looking deeply into dark brown.

'Please do,' he encouraged.

What Bella lacked in experience she hoped she made up for in her delight at being given the freedom to explore the sculptured perfection of Gabriel's mouth in the same way he had hers. She heard his ragged intake of breath as she gently sucked his top lip into her mouth and her tongue slowly licked the heady champagne from that softness. His hand moved up to entangle his fingers into her hair as she gave the same treatment to his bottom lip, knowing as those fingers tightened in her hair that these caresses were arousing Gabriel as deeply as they were her.

Gabriel's body hardened more with each heated sweep of Bella's tongue against his lips, the throb of his thighs becoming an urgent demand. In fact, he wasn't even sure he was going to make it as far as the bedroom before stripping Bella's clothes from her deliciously responsive body and surging hotly, satisfyingly inside her!

He moved back abruptly, a nerve pulsing in his tightly clenched jaw as he stood up to hold out his hand to her. 'Come with me, Bella,' he invited as she looked up at him uncertainly.

Gabriel continued to hold that gaze as Bella placed her hand in his and rose gracefully to her feet, her breasts quickly rising and falling beneath the thin wool of her sweater.

She was like a small, wild thing, Gabriel acknowledged with growing wonder. So tiny. So delicate. So absolutely, potently desirable.

Gabriel felt his stomach muscles tighten with the force of that desire, continuing to keep a firm hold of her delicate fingers as he picked up the chilled bottle of champagne with his other hand, neither of them speaking as they went into his bedroom.

'Please don't…' Bella protested shyly as Gabriel would have turned on the bedside light.

A four-poster bed! A genuine antique if Bella wasn't mistaken, as were the drapes of deep gold brocade that could be pulled around the four sides of the bed.

What did it matter whether or not the bed and drapes were genuinely old? It was still a bed. A bed Bella had no doubts she would shortly be sharing—very shortly, if the heat of his gaze was any indication!—with Gabriel Danti.

This was madness. Sheer, utter, delicious madness!

'I want to be able to look at you as I make love to you, Bella,' Gabriel said, once again standing very close to her, but not touching her, the warmth of his body alone acting on Bella's senses like a drug. 'Will you allow me to do that?' he encouraged throatily. 'I will undress first if you would be more comfortable with that…?'

God knew Bella wanted to look at him in all his naked glory! 'Please do,' she begged breathlessly.

He reached out to turn on the bedside lamp, to bathe the room in a muted golden glow before he reached up and began to unfasten the buttons down the front of his black shirt.

Bella found her gaze fixed on the movements of those long, elegantly slender hands as they slowly slipped each button from its fastening, the silk falling back to reveal the muscled hardness of Gabriel's chest covered in another dusting of dark hair. Dark hair that thickened as it reached his navel before disappearing below the waistband of his black tailored trousers.

It was instinct, pure compulsion that caused Bella to reach out and touch his chest, to feel the tautness of his flesh beneath her fingertips as it stretched tightly across those muscles. His skin felt hot and fevered, those muscles tightening as Bella's hands moved up to slide the shirt from his shoulders before she dropped the garment to the carpeted floor.

Gabriel was as beautiful as the angel he was named

for. Achingly, temptingly gorgeous as his eyes burned hotly in the chiselled beauty of his face.

Bella wanted to see more. Wanted to see all of him!

Her hands trembled slightly as she unfastened his trousers to slide the zip down slowly, her fingers skimming lightly across Gabriel's arousal beneath black underpants, causing him to draw in a sharp breath.

His hand moved down to clasp hers against him. 'Feel how badly I want you, Bella,' he grated fiercely. 'Feel it!'

She looked up at him, their gazes fusing hotly, Bella never more sure of anything in her life as she slowly, deliberately, peeled away Gabriel's last item of clothing to release his pulsing erection.

He was long and thick, incredibly hard, that hardness moving against her hand as Bella reached out to touch him.

Gabriel felt his control slipping, groaning softly, lids closing, his jaw clenching, as his pleasure centred totally on the caress of Bella's fingers against his arousal. Selfishly he wanted those caresses to continue to their pleasurable conclusion. But more than that he wanted to see Bella, to touch her with the same intimacy as she was now touching him.

His gaze held hers as he stepped back slightly before reaching out to grasp the bottom of her thin sweater and draw it slowly up over her breasts and then her head before adding it to the pile of clothes on the carpet. Gabriel's breath caught in his throat as he gazed at the firm thrust of her breasts, the nipples a deep, dusky rose, and a waist so small and slender Gabriel felt sure he would be able to span it with his hands.

He slowly bent his head to kiss those uptilting

breasts, able to see and feel Bella's response as his tongue moved moistly across one nipple before he drew it deeply into his mouth.

Bella was lost. Totally, utterly lost as her hands moved up to clasp Gabriel's head to her, her fingers tangling in the heavy thickness of his hair as the pleasure created by his lips and tongue washed over her in dark, sensuous waves, pooling achingly between her thighs. An ache that Gabriel helped to assuage as his hand moved to cup her there, pressing lightly, Bella gasping weakly as he unerringly found the centre of her arousal.

She had no idea which one of them removed her jeans and panties, any more than she could remember how they came to be lying on the bed, bodies pressed close together, legs entwined as they kissed hotly, fiercely, feverishly.

Bella stopped breathing altogether as Gabriel's hand parted her thighs before his thumb began to touch, to stroke, the hardened nub that nestled there. Her senses became saturated with the intensity of her arousal, her hips rising off the bed to meet the thrust of Gabriel's fingers as they moved deeply, rhythmically inside her and Bella exploded with spasm after spasm of unimagined pleasure, her head moving from side to side on the pillow, her fingers curled into the sheets beneath her as that pleasure seemed never ending.

It didn't end as Gabriel moved above her, his gaze holding hers as he slowly, inch by inch, entered her still quivering body until he claimed her completely. He began to move inside her, his thrusts slow and measured, and then increasing in depth, Gabriel groaning low in his throat as he surged fiercely inside her. Bella met the fierceness of his thrusts as she—amazingly, incredibly!—felt her own release building for a second time in as many minutes.

Her eyes widened, deeply purple, as that release grew, the pleasure so achingly deep now it was almost painful in its intensity as Gabriel deliberately slowed the strokes of his erection inside her, holding her on the edge of that plateau, refusing to release her as he watched her pleasure.

'Please!' Bella gasped restlessly as her body burned and ached for that release. 'Oh, God, please!'

He continued to watch her even as he moved up onto his arms, his thrusts deepening, becoming harder, quicker, his cheeks flushed with his own pleasure, eyes glittering like onyx as Bella's second release took him over that edge with her.

Gabriel closed his eyes at the force of his release, surging, pumping, hot and fierce, his hips continuing to move against Bella's long after he had completely spilled himself as he remained hard inside her and the quivering pleasure still washed over and through him.

Finally, when he could take no more, when he felt as if he would die if the intensity of it didn't stop, Gabriel collapsed weakly onto Bella's breasts, turning only to pull the bedclothes over them both as they fell into a deep, exhausted sleep, their bodies still joined.

'It's time to wake up, Bella.'

Bella was already awake, had woken up several minutes ago in fact, and was trying to come to terms with who she was here with.

Gabriel Danti…

Just thinking of his name conjured up images of the night that had just passed. Of waking up in the early hours of the morning to find Gabriel once more hard inside her, his gaze silently questioning as he looked down at her. A question Bella had silently answered by the slow, languorous thrust of her thighs as her mouth became fused with his.

If anything, the second time they had made love had been even more intense than the first—and Bella hadn't believed that anything could possibly match their first time together!

But, having woken up alone in the four-poster bed a few minutes ago, the sound of the shower running in the adjoining bathroom telling her where Gabriel was, instead of the happy euphoria Bella should have been feeling after such a night of pure pleasure, she had instead been filled with a sense of trepidation.

Last night she had made love with Gabriel Danti. Number one driver of the Formula One racing championship. Playboy son and heir of the Danti business and wine empire.

Whereas she was the eldest daughter of an English country doctor, hopefully with a forthcoming degree in art and history.

Not only that, but Bella knew she was far from the tall, leggy blonde models or actresses that Gabriel usually escorted to the glitzy parties and film premieres he seemed to attend on a regular basis. The glossy magazines were constantly showing photographs of him with those women, most recently the model Janine Childe.

So she and Gabriel had absolutely nothing in common!

Out of the bedroom, that was…

In the cold light of dawn Bella blushed to the roots of her tangled hair as she relived each and every one of their intimate caresses of the night before.

Of course, she should have thought of all the reasons she shouldn't be here with Gabriel before she went to bed with him. She probably would have done so if she hadn't been quite so mesmerised by all that brooding Latin charm. If she hadn't been held in thrall by the hard beauty of Gabriel's face and body…

'Bella…?' Gabriel prompted again as he moved to sit on the side of the bed. 'Wake up, *cara*, so that I can say goodbye properly.'

Goodbye?

Bella's lids flew open wide as she turned her head to look at Gabriel sitting on the bed beside her. She was grateful that she had the sheet draped over her to hide her nakedness when she saw that Gabriel was fully dressed in a black polo shirt that emphasised the width of his shoulders and chest, and faded jeans that rested low down on his hips, his hair still wet from the shower he had just taken.

Gabriel's smile was quizzical as he looked down at Bella, once again fascinated by how beautiful she was. How tiny and curvaceous. How responsive…

He felt his body stir, his thighs hardening, as he recalled just how responsive Bella had been the previous evening and once again during the night. How his own response had been deepened, intensified, to match hers.

He reached out to smooth the fringe of dark hair from her brow, his gaze holding hers as he bent to kiss her, slowly, his expression regretful when he finally raised his head. 'I really do have to go now, Bella, or I am going to be late getting to Silverstone,' he murmured huskily. 'But I will call you later, okay?'

'Okay,' she whispered.

Gabriel stood up reluctantly, as aware of the minutes ticking by as he was of Bella's nakedness beneath the sheet, and knowing he had to remove himself from the temptation she represented. 'My housekeeper will call a taxi for you when you are ready to leave.' He spoke abruptly as he fought the urge he had to say to hell with the practice session and remain here in bed with Bella instead. 'As I cannot drive you home myself I have left you some money on the dressing-table to pay for the taxi,' he added lightly, remembering that Bella had only recently ceased being a student.

She frowned slightly. 'That won't be necessary.'

'Bella…?' Gabriel lowered his own brows darkly as he could read none of her thoughts in those violet-coloured eyes.

'It's fine, Gabriel.' Bella forced a lightness to her tone that was completely contradicted by the heaviness that had settled in her chest at the suddenness of Gabriel's departure.

'I will call you later, Bella,' he repeated firmly. Gabriel bent once again to kiss her on the lips before turning to leave, pausing at the door to turn and add, 'Take your time showering—there is no hurry for you to leave.'

CHAPTER ONE

Five years later...

'As PARTIES go this one is pretty amazi—I don't believe it!' Claudia gasped incredulously.

'What don't you believe?' Bella prompted indulgently, her sister having exclaimed over one wonder or another since the family's arrival in San Francisco two days ago.

Although Bella had to admit that the view of the San Francisco evening skyline from this private function room at the top of one of its most prestigious hotels was pretty spectacular. She could even see the Golden Gate Bridge lit up in all its splendour.

'Wow! I mean—wow!' Claudia wasn't looking out of the window but across the crowded room where the private party, to introduce the two families of their cousin Brian and his American fiancée Dahlia Fabrizzi, was taking place on the eve of their wedding. 'But it can't really be him, can it?' she queried as she frowned. 'Of course Aunt Gloria has been dropping huge hints the last few days about Dahlia's mother being well connected, but, still, I can't believe—'

'Claudia, will you for goodness' sake stop waffling into your champagne and just—?' Bella broke off abruptly as she turned to see who was holding her sister so enrapt, and instantly recognised the 'him' Claudia had to be referring to.

Bella hadn't seen him for five years. Five years! And yet she had no trouble whatsoever in recognising Gabriel Danti!

No! Claudia was right; it couldn't possibly be him, Bella assured herself. Not here, of all places. It had to be an illusion.

Or perhaps just a waking nightmare!

'It *is* him!' Claudia exclaimed excitedly as she clutched Bella's arm. 'It's Gabriel Danti, Bella! Can you believe it?'

No, Bella couldn't believe it. She didn't *want* to believe it!

Maybe it wasn't him, just someone who looked a lot like him?

The height was the same, but the dark hair was much shorter than Bella remembered. The eyes, although dark, were cold and aloof despite the smile that curved those chiselled lips as he was introduced to several other guests. The cleft in the chin was also the same, but this man had a scar running from beneath his left eye to his jaw to mar the harsh, sculptured beauty of his face.

Bella remembered that Gabriel Danti had been photographed sporting a long scar down the left side of his face when he was discharged from hospital three months after the horrendous crash that had put an end to his own racing career and killed two of his fellow drivers.

Months after his accident, Gabriel Danti had returned

to Italy on the family owned jet, had been photographed as he left the hospital, and then again as he entered the plane, but had rarely been seen in public since. His racing career over, he had turned his concentration on the Danti wineries and seemingly retired from the playboy lifestyle he had once so enjoyed.

'Do you remember those posters of him I had stuck all over my bedroom walls when I was younger?' Claudia laughed.

Of course Bella remembered those posters—they had given her the shivers for months following that night Bella had spent with him, her relief immense once Claudia took them down and replaced them with posters of one of the bad-boy actors of Hollywood.

'He's gorgeous, isn't he?' Claudia sighed dreamily.

'Lovely,' Bella answered insincerely, watching the man standing across the crowded room now talking to her uncle Simon.

He was several inches taller than her uncle, and had to bend slightly in order to hear the older man's conversation. He looked dark and mesmerising, his body lithe and obviously fit in the black evening suit and snowy white shirt with a black bow tie.

Could it really be Gabriel?

From the way his mere presence had ensnared the attention of all the female guests at the party Bella could well believe it was him. She just didn't want it to be!

'His hair's shorter, of course— Oh, look, he favours his left leg…' Claudia sympathised as their cousin Brian moved with the man to introduce him to several members of his own family who had made the trip over for the wedding tomorrow..

'His legs were badly crushed in the accident five years ago, remember,' Bella murmured with a frown.

'You would have thought that all the Danti millions could have fixed that,' her sister mused. 'You know, Bella,' she added slowly, 'he reminds me of someone…'

'Probably Gabriel Danti!' Bella said sharply as she finally came out of the dazed stupor that had held her firmly in its grip, linking her arm with her sister's in order to turn Claudia in the direction of the bar. 'Let's go and get some more champagne.'

'Aren't you in the least intrigued to know if it *is* him?' Claudia looked at her teasingly. She was of a similar height to Bella, but her hair was a short, wispy cap of ebony, the blue of her figure-hugging knee-length gown a perfect match in colour for her eyes.

'Not in the least,' Bella dismissed firmly, deliberately going to the farthest end of the bar away from the crowd of people where the man who looked like Gabriel Danti was now the centre of attention, several other people having drifted over to join the group, obviously as intrigued as Claudia.

Claudia gave a husky chuckle of affection as they stood at the bar waiting for their champagne glasses to be refilled. 'My big sister, the man hater!'

Bella raised dark brows. 'I don't hate all men—just those that have gone through puberty!'

'Exactly.' Claudia grinned, her face arrestingly pretty rather than classically beautiful. 'I wonder if I should go over and say hello to Brian and see if he can introduce me to— No, wait a minute…' Her attention noticeably sharpened as she looked over Bella's shoulder. 'I do believe our darling cousin is bringing him over to meet us!' Her face brightened excitedly.

No!

Bella couldn't believe this was happening!

She didn't even want to look at a man who resembled Gabriel Danti, let alone be introduced to him—

'And last, but not least, I would like you to meet the two most beautiful women I know after Dahlia,' Brian said affectionately behind her. 'Bella, Claudi, can I introduce you to Dahlia's cousin, Gabriel Danti? Gabriel, my cousins, Claudia and Isabella Scott.'

It truly *was* Gabriel Danti!

Bella couldn't breathe. Her mind had gone completely blank. Her knees had turned to jelly. In fact no part of her seemed to be functioning properly.

Luckily for her Claudia had eagerly grasped on to the introduction, and was even now enthusing to Gabriel how much she had enjoyed watching him during his career in Formula One racing, giving Bella a little time to catch her breath as she heard the familiar husky accented tones as he murmured a polite but dismissive response.

Perhaps Gabriel wouldn't remember her? Bella thought frantically.

Of course he wouldn't remember her!

Why should he remember the student of art and history called Bella who had once shared his bed for the night?

From his lack of a phone call, she could only assume he had forgotten her instantly!

'Bella…?' Brian prompted lightly as she still kept her back firmly turned towards both him and his guest.

Bella drew in a deep, steadying breath, knowing that

she had no choice but to turn and face the man she so
longed to forget, as he had her.

Gabriel's expression was blandly polite as Isabella Scott
turned to face him. 'Miss Scott,' he greeted evenly as
he briefly took the cool slenderness of her hand in his
before releasing it. 'Or may I call you Isabella?'

'I—'

'Everyone calls her Bella,' Claudia put in helpfully.

'May I?' The icy darkness of Gabriel's gaze easily
held Bella captive.

Violet-coloured eyes were surrounded by thick dark
lashes the same colour as that wild cascade of hair down
the slender length of her spine...

Bella blinked before abruptly breaking the intensity
of Gabriel's gaze to focus on something across the
room. 'Bella is fine,' she answered him evenly.

Isabella Scott looked self-assured and incredibly
beautiful in an off-the-shoulder gown of the exact
colour of her eyes, and, if Gabriel was not mistaken, her
small, pointed chin was slightly raised in challenge as
her gaze returned questioningly to meet the intensity of
his...

'More guests to greet,' Brian Kingston murmured
apologetically as he glanced across the room. 'Excuse
me, won't you, Gabriel? I'm sure Bella and Claudi will
be only too pleased to keep you entertained.' He shot a
teasing glance at the younger of the two cousins before
turning and making his way back across the crowded
room to his fiancée's side.

Gabriel's gaze was hooded as he continued to look
steadily at Bella. 'Will you?'

An irritated frown appeared between her eyes. 'Will I what?' she prompted sharply.

'Be pleased to keep me entertained?' he drawled with cool mockery.

Purple lights flashed in the depths of her eyes. 'Do you need entertaining, Mr Danti?'

'In truth, I doubt I will be staying long enough for that to be necessary,' he conceded.

Gabriel hadn't intended attending this party at all this evening, but at the last moment his father had asked him to represent the Danti side of the family, as he didn't feel well enough to attend the party of his niece this evening as well as her wedding tomorrow. Gabriel had reluctantly agreed to come in his place, his intention to only stay long enough to satisfy the proprieties.

At least, it had been…

Gabriel Danti wasn't staying long, Bella triumphed with inward relief. 'I'm sure Claudia and I can manage a few minutes' polite conversation, Mr Danti.'

Gabriel Danti gave a mocking inclination of his head before turning his attention to Claudia. 'Are you enjoying your visit to San Francisco, Claudia?'

Bella allowed her breath to leave her lungs in a soft, shaky sigh as she at last felt herself released from the intensity of Gabriel's dark, compelling gaze, and she took those few moments of respite to study him more closely.

The man she had met five years ago had possessed the broodingly magnetic good looks of his heavenly namesake. Along with a lazy self-confidence and charm that was utterly captivating, and a warm sensuality in those chocolate-brown eyes that undressed a woman at a glance.

Or, in Bella's experience, made a woman want to undress for him at a glance!

The man talking oh-so-politely to Claudia still possessed those broodingly magnetic good looks—the livid scar down the left side of his face only added a dangerous edge to that attraction!—but his eyes were no longer that warm and sensual colour of melted chocolate but were instead a flat, unemotional brown, and the lazy charm and self-confidence had been replaced with a cold and arrogant aloofness.

As far as Bella was aware, Gabriel had never married—although, in all honesty, Bella hadn't particularly gone out of her way to learn anything about his life in the five years since they had parted so abruptly.

What would have been the point? The two of them had shared nothing more than a night of unimaginable and unrepeatable passion.

'Would you care for a drink?'

Bella raised startled eyes to Gabriel's, frowning slightly as she saw the glass he held out to her. Champagne. It would have to be champagne, wouldn't it?

'Thank you,' she accepted stiltedly.

Gabriel watched beneath hooded lids as Bella's cheeks warmed with colour as she took the fluted glass from him with a deftness that prevented her fingers from coming into contact with his.

His mouth twisted derisively as he asked, 'Is this your first visit to San Francisco, too, Bella?'

'Yes.'

'You like the city?'

'Very much.'

'Have you done much sightseeing since your arrival?'

'Some, yes.'

Gabriel's gaze narrowed at the economy of her replies. 'Perhaps—'

'Excuse me for interrupting, Gabriel,' his cousin Dahlia, tomorrow's bride, cut in lightly as she joined them, 'but my brother Benito is anxious to become re-acquainted with Claudia,' she added indulgently.

'Really?' The younger of the two Scott sisters glanced across the room to where Benito stood watching her intently.

Bella felt herself begin to tremble as she was overwhelmed with an impending sense of doom. If Claudia left then Bella would be completely alone with—

'You don't mind, do you, Bella?' Claudia's eyes were glowing with excitement. She had confided in Bella earlier today, after being introduced to Benito the previous evening, that she definitely wanted to get to know Dahlia's older brother better.

Obviously the attraction was reciprocated—which didn't help Bella in the least when she had no inclination whatsoever to be left alone with Gabriel Danti!

'I assure you, Claudia, your sister will be perfectly safe with me,' Gabriel replied with dry mockery before Bella had a chance to say anything.

Bella shot him a glance beneath her long lashes. She still had absolutely no idea whether or not Gabriel remembered her from their night together five years ago—and she didn't want to know, either.

She remembered *him*, and that was bad enough!

But before she could add anything to his reply Claudia gave her arm a grateful squeeze. 'Thanks, Bella,' she whispered before moving away to accompany Dahlia over to where the dark and handsome Benito stood waiting.

The sudden silence the two women left in their wake seemed deafening to Bella.

The room was full of people, at least a hundred or so of the guests invited to the wedding tomorrow, all of them chatting or laughing as they either renewed old acquaintances or met new ones. And yet as far as Bella was concerned she and Gabriel could have been alone on an island in the Arctic—the air between them was certainly frigidly cold enough for them to be on one!

'There is a more—private sitting area next to this one in which we might talk,' Gabriel bit out abruptly.

Bella raised apprehensive eyes, knowing that wariness was justified as Gabriel looked down his nose at her with a glacial brown gaze, his mouth—the mouth she had once found so sensually mesmerising!—flattened to a thin, uncompromising line above that cleft chin.

She moistened suddenly dry lips. 'I'm perfectly happy where I am, thank you, Mr Danti.'

His eyes became even more icy as he reached out and curled his fingers compellingly about the top of her arm. 'It was a statement of intent, Bella, not a question,' he assured her grimly as he began to walk towards the exit, Bella firmly anchored to his side, the stiffness of his left leg barely noticeable.

'But—'

'Do you really want to have this conversation here, in front of Dahlia and Brian's other guests?' he asked harshly as he came to a halt halfway across the crowded room to look down at her through narrowed lids.

Bella swallowed hard as she saw the unmistakeably

angry glitter in that dark gaze. 'I have absolutely no idea what conversation you're referring to—'

'Oh, I think that you do, Bella,' he retorted menacingly.

Bella thought that she did, too!

She only wished that she didn't. But Gabriel's behaviour since Claudia and Dahlia's departure all pointed to the fact that he *did* remember her from five years ago, after all…

CHAPTER TWO

'I REALLY have no idea what the two of us could possibly have to talk about, Mr Danti,' Bella told him stiltedly as he sat perfectly relaxed in the armchair across from hers in the quiet of the otherwise deserted small reception-room just down the hallway from where the family party was being held.

Gabriel's eyes narrowed on the paleness of her face as she sat stiffly upright in her own chair. 'Considering our—past acquaintance, shall we say?—I believe refraining from addressing me as "Mr Danti" in that superior tone would be a good way to begin.'

She raised her brows in what she hoped was a querying manner. 'Our past acquaintance…?'

Gabriel's mouth thinned. 'Do not play games with me, Bella!'

She shot him another glance before looking sharply away again. 'I wasn't sure you had remembered we'd met before…'

'Oh, I remember,' he growled.

She swallowed hard before speaking. 'As do I— Gabriel,' she conceded tightly.

He gave a humourless smile. 'You had absolutely no idea I would be here tonight, did you?'

Those eyes flashed deeply purple at his mocking tone. 'Why should I have done? Dahlia's name is Fabrizzi.'

'Her mother, my aunt Teresa, is my father's younger sister,' Gabriel supplied evenly.

Bella's mouth twisted. 'How sweet that you flew all the way from Italy to attend your cousin's wedding!'

Gabriel's mouth thinned at her obvious mockery. 'I no longer live in Italy, Bella.'

She looked startled. 'You don't?'

Gabriel shook his head. 'I spend most of my time at the Danti vineyards about an hour's drive away from here, but I also have a house right here in San Francisco.'

Bella could easily guess exactly where in San Francisco that house was!

She and the rest of her family had gone for a tour of the city earlier today, and part of that tour had been through an area known as Pacific Heights, where the houses were grand and gracious—and worth millions of dollars!

'Do you like living in America?' she asked curiously.

Gabriel shrugged. 'It has its—advantages.'

Bella just bet that it did! She also couldn't help wondering if Gabriel's move to America didn't have something to do with the fact that Janine Childe, the woman Gabriel had once been in love with—perhaps was still in love with?—now lived in California, too...

'Have you now finished with the polite exchange of information?' Gabriel asked.

Bella forced her gaze to remain level on his. 'What do you want from me, Gabriel?'

What did he want from her? That was an interesting question, Gabriel acknowledged grimly. Until he had arrived at the party earlier, and seen Bella across the room as she chatted with the young woman he now knew to be her sister, Gabriel would have liked to believe he had cast Bella from his mind after that single night together. But having recognised her instantly, he knew he could no longer claim that to be the case…

If anything, Isabella Scott was even more strikingly lovely than she had been five years ago, maturity having added self-assurance to a beauty that had already been breathtaking. Her violet eyes were still as stunning as ever, her hair was still long and the colour of ebony, but styled now in heavy layers so that it swung silkily against her cheeks and her throat, before cascading wildly down the length of her back. And the close fit of her violet gown revealed that her waist was still delicately slender beneath the full thrust of those perfect breasts…

What did he want from her?

He wanted not to have noticed any of those things!

His mouth set in a grim, uncompromising line. 'What do you have to give, Bella?'

Her gaze was searching as she eyed him warily, and Gabriel knew that Bella would see that he, at least, was visibly much changed from their last meeting.

The darkness of his hair was styled several inches shorter than it had once been, but the scar that ran the length of his left cheek—a constant reminder, when Gabriel looked in the mirror to shave each morning, of the guilt he carried inside—was a much more visible reminder of how much he had changed in the last five years.

Was Bella repulsed, as Gabriel was himself, by the livid ugliness of that scar?

'What do I have to give to you, in particular?' Bella repeated incredulously. 'Absolutely nothing!' she scornfully answered her own question.

Gabriel's hand moved instinctively to the jagged wound that marred his cheek. 'That, at least, has not changed,' he rasped coldly.

Bella eyed him frowningly. Why was he looking at her so contemptuously? He was the one who had seduced her only because the woman he had really wanted—the beautiful supermodel, Janine Childe— had told him their relationship was over, and that she was involved with one his fellow Formula One drivers.

That Formula One driver had been Paulo Descari. Killed in the crash that had occurred only hours after Gabriel had left Bella in his bed.

Janine Childe had tearfully claimed at the time that Gabriel had deliberately caused the accident out of jealousy, because of Paulo Descari's relationship with her.

While not convinced Gabriel would have deliberately caused that crash, five years later Bella still cringed whenever she thought that being on the rebound had been Gabriel's only reason for spending the night with her.

So how dared Gabriel now look at her with such contempt?

'I've changed, Gabriel,' she told him pointedly.

'For the better?'

Bella frowned. 'What the—'

'Did you ever marry, Bella?' Gabriel cut icily across her protest, his mouth twisting derisively as his dark gaze moved over the bareness of her left hand. 'I see not. Perhaps that is as well,' he added insultingly.

Bella took an outraged breath. 'Perhaps it's as well that you have never married either!' She came back in just as cutting a tone.

He gave a humourless smile. 'Perhaps.'

'I don't think the two of us sitting here exchanging insults is in the least harmonious to Brian and Dahlia's wedding tomorrow, do you?' she challenged.

Bella's heart sank every time she thought of attending that wedding.

She had been looking forward for weeks to this trip to San Francisco. But meeting Gabriel again, knowing he was going to be at the wedding tomorrow, too, now made it an ordeal Bella didn't even want to attempt to get through.

But she had no idea how to get out of it, either...

Gabriel watched the emotions as they flickered across Bella's beautiful and expressive face, taking a guess at the reason for her look of trepidation. 'Your parents and brother are here for the wedding also?'

'Yes,' she confirmed quietly.

He gave a ruthless smile. 'And they, like your sister just now, have no idea that the two of us have ever met before.' It was a statement, not a question.

'No,' she sighed.

Gabriel gave a mocking inclination of his head. 'And you would prefer that it remain that way?'

Bella sent him a narrow-eyed glance. 'Yes!'

'They would not understand our having spent the night together five years ago?'

'*I* don't understand it, so why should they!' Bella exclaimed. 'That night was totally out of character for me. Totally,' she added vehemently as she remembered just how eager, how *gullible* she had been.

Gabriel almost felt a hint of sympathy for Bella as he noticed that her hands were trembling slightly as she wrapped her fingers about her fluted glass sitting on the table in front of her. Almost. The fact it was champagne that bubbled inside the glass, the same wine that Gabriel had once dribbled all over this woman's body, before slowly licking it from the sensuous softness of her skin, precluded him feeling in the least sorry for Bella's obvious discomfort with this unexpected encounter.

He shrugged unsympathetically. 'I am sure that we all have things in our past that we wish had not happened.'

Bella wondered briefly if he could possibly be talking about that horrific car crash and Janine Childe's accusations, but then she saw the hard glitter in Gabriel's eyes as he looked at her, and the contemptuous curl of his top lip, and Bella realised he had been referring to her, that she was something he wished had not happened in his life, either.

She swallowed before speaking. 'Then we're both agreed that it would be better for everyone if we both just forgot our—past acquaintance?' She deliberately used his own description of that night five years ago.

The grimness of his smile lacked any genuine humour. 'If only it were that simple, Bella…'

If only.

But it wasn't. Bella, more than anyone, knew that it wasn't.

Much as she hated meeting Gabriel again like this, let alone having to sit through this insulting conversation, she also thanked God that this initial meeting had taken place this evening. It could have been so much more disastrous if it had happened at the wedding tomorrow instead…

She straightened, pushing her wine glass away from her so that she didn't risk knocking it over. 'Let's make it that simple, Gabriel,' she offered. 'We'll both just agree to stay well away from each other for the rest of my stay in San Francisco.' Which was only three more days, thank goodness; her father hadn't been able to take any longer than a week away from his medical practice.

Gabriel's gaze narrowed as he took in the smooth creaminess of Bella's skin as she flicked her hair back over her shoulders. Deliberately drawing attention to the full swell of her breasts above the fitted purple gown? Somehow, going on their previous conversation, Gabriel didn't think so.

'One dance together, Bella, and then perhaps I will consider your suggestion,' he murmured huskily.

Her eyes widened. 'One dance?'

'They have begun dancing at the party now that all of the guests have arrived,' he pointed out dryly, the earlier soft strains of background music having given way to louder dance music.

Bella looked confused. 'You want to *dance* with me?'

'Why not?' Gabriel wanted to know.

Her cheeks were very pale. 'Because—well, because—Can you dance? I mean—'

'You mean considering I am so obviously disadvantaged?' Gabriel rasped harshly, his expression grim as he acknowledged that she had obviously noticed that, as well as the scar on his face, he also favoured his left leg when he walked.

Not that the disability was anywhere near as bad as it had been five years ago. Gabriel had spent several months in a wheelchair after the accident, several more painful months after that learning to walk again. That he now had the scar and a slight limp as the only visible sign of the car crash, even if unsightly, was a miracle.

Bella gave an impatient shake of her head. 'You're about as *disadvantaged* as a stalking tiger!'

'I am pleased that you realise that,' he growled—and had the satisfaction of seeing the heated colour that instantly flooded her cheeks. 'I am definitely able to dance, Bella. As long as the music is slow,' he added challengingly.

Slow…! Bella inwardly groaned. What Gabriel really meant by that was he could dance to the sort of music where a man held the woman closely in his arms… Her mouth firmed. 'I was actually thinking of excusing myself and going to bed—'

'Was that an invitation for me to join you?' he smoothly inserted.

'No, it most certainly was not!' She flushed slightly as she almost screeched her indignation with the suggestion. Definitely an overreaction to that sort of temptation…

He shrugged. 'Then I believe I will return to the

party once you have left and ask that Brian introduce me to your parents.'

Bella glared across the table at him. 'You rat! You absolute, unmitigated—'

'I will tolerate the name calling once, Bella.' Gabriel's tone was steely. 'But only once,' he warned coldly. 'It is your choice.' Then his tone softened almost to pleasantness as he relaxed back in his chair to once again look across at her with mocking eyes. 'Consent to one dance with me or I will ask to meet your parents.'

'Why?' she groaned protestingly. 'Why do you even want to dance with me?'

'Curiosity, perhaps…?'

'Curiosity about what?' She voiced her bewilderment.

His gaze roamed over her slowly, from the darkness of her hair, across her face, and then lower, to the swell of her breasts.

Bella could barely breathe as she suffered that slow perusal, rising abruptly to her feet when she could no longer bear the deliberate insult of that gaze. 'One dance, Gabriel,' she said, abruptly giving in. 'After which, I would prefer it if you didn't so much as speak to me again!'

He smiled before rising more leisurely to his feet. 'I will let you know how I feel about that after we have danced together.'

Bella shrugged off the hold Gabriel would have taken of her arm, instead walking several feet away from him as they returned down the hallway to the function room where the party was being held.

She was nevertheless aware of everything about him,

from the mocking gleam in those dark eyes, the smile of satisfaction that curved those sculptured lips and that sexy cleft in the centre of his arrogant chin, to the lithe grace of his body as he easily compensated for the injury he had sustained in the crash five years ago.

According to the newspaper reports at the time, Gabriel's injuries had been horrific. Both legs and his pelvis crushed. Burns over much of his torso. Numerous cuts on his body, the worst of them that terrible gash to his left cheek. But as far as Bella was concerned, those scars only added to the air of danger Gabriel had already possessed in such abundance!

'Perfect,' Gabriel murmured with satisfaction when a slow ballad began to play as they entered the crowded function room. The lights had been dimmed and several couples were already dancing in the space that had been cleared in the centre of the room, including Claudia Scott and his cousin Benito. 'A pity there is not a song about a lady in purple,' Gabriel mocked, taking hold of Bella's hand as they stepped onto the dance floor.

'I would prefer it if we danced formally,' she told Gabriel stiffly as he deliberately placed his arms about her waist to draw her against him, her hands crushed against his chest.

'Did no one ever tell you that life is full of disappointments?' he murmured, a hand against her spine continuing to hold her body moulded against his as they began to move slowly in time to the music.

She pulled back slightly, her eyes glittering with anger. 'Oh, yes,' she snapped scathingly. 'Someone taught me that only too well!'

Gabriel raised dark brows. 'Then it will not surprise

you to know that I prefer that we continue to dance exactly as we are.'

Bella was past being surprised by anything that happened this evening!

In fact, she was too busy fighting her complete awareness of the hardness of Gabriel's body pressed so close to her own, his cheek resting lightly against her hair, the warmth of his hand against her spine, his other hand enveloping one of her own as he held it against his chest, to be able to concentrate on anything else.

Much as she wished it weren't so, Bella was aware of everything about Gabriel as they danced. His heat. His smell. The warmth of his breath against her temple. The sensuality of his body against hers as he moved them both to the slow beat of the music.

And Bella was also supremely aware of her own response to all of those things, her breathing soft and uneven, her skin sensitised, her breasts swelling, the nipples hardening, and a deep hot ache pooling between her thighs.

This was torture. Absolute torture.

Nor was her discomfort helped by the fact that Claudia had spotted the two of them dancing so closely together, her encouraging nods and smiles showing Bella that one member of her family, at least, was totally fooled by Gabriel's marked interest in her.

Bella pulled slightly away from him, releasing her hand from his as she deliberately put several inches between them. 'I think we've danced quite long enough, don't you?' she said stiffly, her gaze fixed on the third button of his white evening shirt.

Gabriel's mouth tightened, his gaze becoming glacial

as he inwardly acknowledged that he had definitely danced with Isabella Scott 'quite long enough'. Long enough for him to confirm that his body still responded to the voluptuousness of Bella's breasts and the warmth of her thighs pressed against his. Which was all he had wanted to know…

'Perhaps you are right,' he said and immediately stepped away from her in the middle of the dance floor.

Bella looked uncomfortable at his abrupt withdrawal, and she glanced about them self-consciously as several of the other people dancing gave them curious glances. 'You're deliberately trying to embarrass me,' she muttered irritably before she turned and walked off the dance floor, her cheeks warm with colour.

'You expressed a wish that we stop dancing.' Gabriel followed at a more leisurely pace.

'Go away, Gabriel. Just *go away*,' she repeated wearily.

Gabriel looked down at her searchingly, the glitter in those purple eyes no longer looking as if it was caused by anger. 'Are you *crying*, Bella?'

'Of course I'm not crying,' she snapped, her chin once again rising in challenge as she now met his gaze defiantly. 'It would take more than the misfortune of having met you again to make me cry!' she said scathingly. 'Now, if you will excuse me? I really would like to go to my room.'

He raised dark brows. 'You are staying here at the hotel?' It was a possibility that hadn't occurred to him.

Her eyes narrowed. 'And so what if I am?'

'I was just curious, Bella,' he pointed out.

'Are you?' She gave a mocking smile. 'I don't remember you being curious enough five years ago to be interested in anyone but yourself.'

Gabriel's mouth thinned warningly. 'Are you accusing me of having been a selfish lover?' He sounded outraged.

'No, of course not!' Bella's cheeks blazed with colour. 'This is a ridiculous conversation!' she added resentfully. 'It's time I was leaving. I won't say it's been a pleasure meeting you again, Gabriel—because we both know that isn't true!' she added before turning and walking away, her head held high.

Gabriel watched Bella as she crossed the room to make her excuses to his aunt and uncle before leaving, her hair long and gloriously silky down the length of her spine, the movements of her hips provocative beneath the purple gown, her legs appearing slender and shapely above the high heels of her purple sandals.

No, Gabriel agreed, it had certainly not been a pleasure to meet Isabella Scott again.

But it had been something…

Bella forced herself to move slowly, calmly, as she made her excuses to her hosts, Teresa and Pablo Fabrizzi, before leaving the function room to walk down the hallway to the lift, refusing to give Gabriel Danti the satisfaction of seeing her hurrying down that hallway in order to escape being the focus of his intense gaze.

She breathed easier once inside the lift, leaning weakly against one of the mirrored walls as she pressed the button to descend to the sixth floor where her room was situated.

Could anything worse than Gabriel Danti being related to her cousin's fiancée possibly have happened?

Bella couldn't think of anything.

Nor had she yet been able to think of a way to avoid being at the wedding tomorrow. But she would have to come up with something. She had to.

'You're back early,' Angela, Dahlia's younger sister, greeted warmly as Bella let herself into the sitting-room of the suite she was sharing with her siblings.

Bella put her evening bag down on the table just inside the door. 'I have a bit of a headache,' she dismissed.

'That's a pity.' Angela stood up, as tall and lithely beautiful as her older sister.

'I also thought that you've been babysitting long enough this evening and perhaps you might like to go up and join in the party for a while?' Bella added warmly, Angela having very kindly offered to take the half a dozen younger members of the English contingent of the wedding party out to a pizza restaurant for the evening, before bringing them back to the hotel and ensuring they all settled down in bed for the night.

'If you're sure you don't mind?' Angela smiled.

'Not at all,' Bella assured her. 'The dancing has only just started,' she added encouragingly.

'Take something for that headache, hmm?' Angela encouraged lightly before letting herself out of the suite.

Bella heaved a shaky sigh, taking several minutes to calm herself before going into the adjoining bedroom where her young brother lay in bed, the bedside lamp still on as he read a book. 'Everything okay, Liam?' she enquired softly as she paused beside him.

Her twelve-year-old brother grinned up at her. 'Fast asleep, as you can see.'

Bella turned, her expression softening as she looked down at the occupant of the second bed.

Her four-year-old son, Toby.

His curls were dark against the pillow, lashes of the same warm chocolate resting on his baby cheeks, his lips slightly parted as he breathed deeply, an endearing dimple in the centre of his chin.

A dimple that Bella knew would one day become a firm cleft.

Just like the one in his father's chin.

CHAPTER THREE

'YOU do not feel a woman's usual need to cry at weddings?'

Bella's back stiffened at the softly taunting sound of Gabriel's voice directly behind her as she stood with all the other wedding guests outside the church, watching the bride and groom as they posed for numerous photographs.

Hard as Bella had tried to find a reason for Toby and herself not to attend the wedding today, including a headache for herself and possible signs of a fever for Toby, ultimately she had had no choice but to concede defeat when her father had declared them both fit and well. Other than throwing herself down a flight of stairs, Bella knew she had lost that particular battle! The most she had been able to hope for was that Gabriel Danti would heed her advice from last night and just stay away from her.

The fact that he was standing behind her now showed that he hadn't!

Bella had seen him when she and the rest of her family arrived for the wedding an hour or so ago, seated in a pew further down the church. Sitting next to him was a silver-haired man whose height and facial likeness to Gabriel indicated that this was probably his father, the aristocratic Cristo Danti.

Her heart had given a jolt as she watched the two Italians unobserved before glancing down at the small boy fidgeting on the pew beside her, instantly recognising how like his father and grandfather Toby was.

As Claudia had also innocently noted the previous evening when she remarked that Gabriel reminded her of someone…!

Thank goodness Toby had disappeared with his adored uncle Liam once the service was over, and was even now playing beneath an oak tree further down the churchyard, with the group of children who had gone out for pizza the evening before.

A fact Bella took note of before she slowly turned to face Gabriel, her response to how handsome he looked in a tailored dark suit and snowy white shirt hidden behind a deliberately neutral expression as she rather wickedly responded to his comment about women usually crying at weddings. 'I'd only cry in sympathy, I'm afraid!'

Gabriel gave an appreciative smile as his hooded gaze swept admiringly over her in the knee-length dress that fitted smoothly over the curves of her slender body, a silk flower pinned behind her left ear and holding back the long length of her dark hair.

She looked cool and beautiful—and utterly self-contained.

It was an assurance that Gabriel perversely wanted to shatter. 'Perhaps that is because no man has so far asked you to become his bride?' he taunted.

Delicate colour warmed her cheeks at the intended insult. 'What on earth makes you assume that, Gabriel?' she retorted. 'Maybe I've simply chosen not to marry because I'm only too aware of how fickle a man's interest can be?' she added sweetly.

Gabriel's mouth thinned at her riposte. 'Perhaps you have been—*meeting* the wrong men…?'

'Perhaps I have.' Her gaze was openly challenging now as it met his.

Enjoyable as it was, this constant bickering with Bella would not do, Gabriel recognised ruefully. It was his cousin's wedding day, an entirely inappropriate time for open dissent between two of her guests.

Bella had obviously come to the same conclusion. 'If you'll excuse me, Gabriel? I have to rejoin my family—' She looked up at Gabriel with sharp enquiry as the fingers he had placed about her arm prevented her from leaving.

A nerve pulsed in his jaw as he looked down at her. 'We need to talk, Bella.'

'We talked yesterday evening, Gabriel—for all the good it did either of us!' she exclaimed.

'Exactly,' he agreed. 'We cannot possibly continue this estrangement between us, when our two families are now united—'

Bella's unamused laugh cut him off. 'My cousin is now married to your cousin—that hardly makes our families united!' she pointed out impatiently. 'In fact, I can't think of another occasion when the two of us will ever have to meet again!'

It was what Bella fervently hoped, at least. At the moment she would just think herself lucky if she could get through the rest of today without this whole situation blowing up in her face.

It really was unfortunate that her father happened to be a doctor, and as such perfectly able to dismiss the illnesses Bella had imagined earlier for both herself and Toby. Although, her previously mythical headache was rapidly becoming a reality during this latest conversation with Gabriel!

How could it be otherwise when she still had absolutely no idea how she was going to prevent Toby and Gabriel from coming face to face at some time during the wedding reception? If that should happen Bella had no idea what Gabriel's reaction would be… After his rejection of her, there was no way she was going to risk Toby being rejected, too, and Gabriel's menacing looks did nothing to calm her fears.

She glanced past Gabriel now as she easily recognised the sound of her young son's giggle, knowing the reason for his joyful laughter as she saw that Liam was tickling him.

Toby was a happy child, totally secure in the adoration of his mother and his indulgent grandparents, as well as his doting aunt and uncle. And Bella wished for him to remain that way.

The last three days had shown her how close the members of the Danti family were, how much they valued and loved their children. She literally quailed at the thought of what Gabriel might do if he were to ever realise that Toby was the result of their single night together five years ago, and how much of his young son's life he'd already missed out on…

'I really do have to go, Gabriel.' Her gaze avoided

meeting his now as she stepped away from him to release herself from his hold on her arm.

Gabriel watched Bella with frowning intensity as she walked away from him, that frown turning to a scowl as he heard the softness of her laughter as she was surrounded by the group of laughing children, some of them the offspring of his own cousins, the likeness to Bella of the tallest of the group making him easily recognisable as her brother Liam.

How strange it was that the people she had talked of so affectionately five years ago—her parents, her sister Claudia and her brother Liam—should now be a reality to him.

'A friend of yours…?'

Gabriel's smile stayed in place as he turned to face his father, revealing none of his inner concern as he saw the unhealthy grey pallor to the older man's face. 'I doubt Bella would think so,' he answered wryly.

'Bella?' Cristo raised silver brows before he glanced across to where Bella was now walking down the pathway chatting with her brother and another of the children.

'Isabella Scott. I met her yesterday evening at Dahlia's party,' Gabriel enlarged.

Again, he could have added. But didn't, knowing that to do so would only arouse his father's insatiable curiosity.

Cristo was the patriarch of the Danti family, and, at sixty-five and ill in health, he had begun to make definite murmurings about Gabriel marrying and producing children to continue the dynasty that Gabriel's great-grandfather had begun with the vineyards in Italy a hundred years ago, and which each succeeding generation had added to. It was Gabriel's own grandfather who had instigated the planting of the vineyards in America seventy years ago.

Gabriel had taken over the running of the California vineyards four years ago, after his father suffered a minor heart attack. But, at the age of thirty-three, unhappily for his father, Gabriel as yet felt no inclination to marry and produce the heirs necessary to continue that dynasty.

As a consequence, Cristo tended to look at every woman Gabriel so much as spoke to as a possible mother to his grandchildren.

How Bella Scott would have laughed if she had known Cristo had briefly considered her for that role!

Bella began to breathe a little easier once the wedding breakfast and speeches were over, and the guests began to wander through to the adjoining room where the evening's dancing was to begin and the socialising to continue. Giving her an ideal opportunity, she hoped, in which to excuse herself and Toby.

Her luck in keeping Toby well away from Gabriel had held during the reception, with Gabriel and his father seated at a dining-table on the furthest side of the room from where Bella sat with her own family.

Dahlia's family being Italian, there were a lot of children present, and the happy couple had chosen to seat all the children at four tables separate from their parents, both allowing the children the freedom to be themselves, and the parents to eat their meal in peace and enjoy socialising with the other adults. This arrangement had also made it impossible to know which children belonged to which parents.

Or, in Bella's case, which parent…

Taking a quick mental note of Gabriel's presence on the other side of the reception room, Bella made her excuses to her own family before slowly making her way towards the door where Dahlia and Brian stood greeting the last of their evening guests, her intention to collect Toby from where he was running riot with the other children, before making—hopefully!—an unnoticed exit.

'You are leaving so soon, Bella?'

She had counted her chickens far too early, Bella acknowledged with a sinking sensation in the pit of her stomach, looking up to see Gabriel Danti's challenging expression as he blocked her progress to the door. 'I have a headache,' she excused tightly.

He raised a mocking eyebrow. 'Weddings really do not agree with you, do they?'

'It's only the prospect of ever having to attend one of my own that I'm allergic to,' she assured him dryly.

Gabriel gave an appreciative smile. He had watched narrow-eyed as Bella made slow but determined progress down the room as she took her leave of several of the other guests, easily guessing that it was her intention to leave early.

It amused him to challenge that departure. 'I trust my own presence has not added to your—discomfort?'

'Not at all.' Those violet-coloured eyes gazed steadily into his. 'My headache is probably a delayed reaction to jet lag.'

'Of course,' Gabriel drawled. 'My father expressed a wish earlier to be introduced to you,' he added not quite truthfully.

No doubt his father would enjoy the introduction, and would draw his own—erroneous—conclusions about it, but he certainly hadn't asked for it.

'Your father?' Bella looked startled by the suggestion. 'Oh, I don't think so, Gabriel—I mean—what would be the point?' she concluded, obviously flustered.

Gabriel studied her beneath hooded lids. 'Politeness, perhaps?' he suggested blandly. 'He is, after all, now the uncle-in-law of your cousin.'

Bella didn't look convinced by that argument. 'As I told you earlier, it's doubtful that any of us will ever meet up again after today.'

He raised dark brows. 'Not even at the christening of Dahlia and Brian's first child?'

Bella hadn't thought of that! This situation really was getting extremely complicated. So much so that she wasn't sure how much longer Gabriel would remain in ignorance of the fact that she had a small son—or, more crucially, that he had one, too!

Nevertheless, she didn't feel able to make that explanation right now, so... 'That's probably years away,' she dismissed sharply. 'Who knows what any of us will be doing then?'

Personally, Bella was thinking of emigrating to Tasmania!

She tried again. 'I really do have to go, Gabriel—'

'Perhaps, as you obviously do not feel inclined to meet my father this evening, you and your family might like to visit the Danti vineyards tomorrow?'

Bella froze, a frown on her brow as she turned to look up at Gabriel with uncertain eyes. 'Why are you doing this?' she asked.

'I merely asked if you and your family would care to come to the Danti vineyards tomorrow,' he reiterated.

'You didn't "merely ask" anything, Gabriel, and you know it,' she argued. 'Just as you know that you are the very last man I wish to spend any more time with!' She was trying not to breathe hard, hoping to conceal the worst of her agitation from him.

'The very last man?' he repeated softly, eyes narrowed suspiciously. 'Why is that, Bella? What did I do to merit such a distinction? Or perhaps it is my scars that you now find so repulsive?' he added harshly.

'I'm insulted that you believe me to be so shallow,' Bella snapped to hide the fact that she had made yet another mistake where this man was concerned.

Yet when had she ever done anything else…?

Toby hadn't been a mistake!

Bella had been stunned five years ago, and not a little frightened, when she'd realised she was pregnant. But that shock and fear had quickly given way to the wonder of the new life growing inside her. Her parents' support, as well as that of Claudia and Liam, had also helped. Especially in the early months when Bella had wondered what she was going to do, how she was going to cope, and especially how she would be able to earn a living once she had a small baby to care for.

Again her parents had been wonderful, insisting that Bella remain living at home with them during her pregnancy, and for some time after Toby was born, by which time Bella had been earning enough money to be able to support them both.

Her parents' attitude to her pregnancy was doubly

admirable when Bella considered that they had done all of that without her ever telling them, or their insisting, on knowing the name of her baby's father…

But how long would they remain in ignorance of his identity if Gabriel went ahead with his intention of inviting her family to the Danti vineyards tomorrow?

She looked at Gabriel searchingly, easily noting his similarity to Toby: the darkness of his hair, the same facial structure, those dark eyes, the cleft in his chin. But was Bella only seeing those similarities because she knew of Toby's paternity? Would her parents, her siblings, see them, too?

Claudia had already seen Gabriel's likeness to 'someone', so Bella obviously couldn't risk it!

'Okay, Gabriel, I'll stay long enough for you to introduce me to your father,' she capitulated suddenly, before turning and preceding him across the room to where Cristo Danti sat in conversation with his sister.

Bella hadn't completely answered his question about being put off by his scar, Gabriel noted with a scowl as he closely followed her to make sure she didn't manage to slip away. But there had been no doubting the vehemence of her claim that he was the very last man she wished to spend any more time with.

Interestingly, Gabriel had once felt exactly the same way about Bella…

His father broke off his conversation and stood up at their approach, Gabriel frowning slightly as he noted the increased pallor in his father's face. The long flight from Italy earlier in the week, and attending Dahlia's wedding today, had obviously taken more of a toll on his father's health than was wise.

Gabriel would suggest that the two of them leave, too, once the introductions were over. 'Papa, may I present Isabella Scott? Bella, my father, Cristo Danti.'

Bella's breath caught in her throat as she looked up into that stern, aristocratic face that was so much like Gabriel's. So much like Toby's, too…

'Mr Danti,' she greeted with a coolness she was far from feeling, only her cheeks echoing her inner warmth as the older man took her hand in his before raising it gallantly to his lips.

'You are well named, Miss Scott,' Cristo Danti murmured appreciatively as he slowly released her hand.

Bella gave an awkward smile. 'Thank you.'

'You are enjoying your stay in San Francisco?'

'Very much, thank you.'

He nodded. 'I have always liked San Francisco.'

'It's certainly an interesting city,' Bella came back non-committally, very aware of Gabriel's broodingly silent presence beside her.

No doubt he was enjoying her discomfort in this stilted conversation with his father. Just as he had enjoyed being able to force this introduction on her in the first place by the veiled threat of inviting her family to the Danti vineyards when she so obviously didn't want his company at all.

'It was a beautiful wedding,' Cristo Danti continued lightly.

'Bella does not enjoy weddings.' Gabriel spoke for the first time. Dryly. Dark brows raised mockingly as Bella shot him a frowning glance.

Bella gave him another quelling glance before answering the older man. 'Dahlia is a lovely bride.'

'Yes, she is.' Cristo Danti's expression was slightly quizzical now as he glanced at his son and then back to Bella. 'Are you remaining in San Francisco long, Miss Scott?'

'Just another couple of days. And please call me Bella,' she invited.

The older man nodded. 'Perhaps before you leave you might care to—'

'Mummy, Nanny and Grandad said we're leaving now!' Toby complained irritably as he suddenly appeared at her side, the excitement of the last week, and his late night yesterday evening, obviously making him tired and slightly querulous.

Bella froze at the first sound of her son's voice, like a nocturnal animal caught in the headlights of an oncoming car.

This couldn't be happening! Not here. Not now!

Bella couldn't breathe. She couldn't move. Couldn't speak.

This was worse than anything she could ever have imagined. Worse than any of the nightmares that had plagued her dreams since she had met Gabriel again yesterday evening.

'*Mummy?*' Gabriel echoed beside her with soft incredulity.

Bella forced herself to move as she slowly turned to look at him, the colour draining from her cheeks as she saw the way he was staring down so intently at Toby.

But it was Cristo Danti, the man standing at Bella's other side, who broke their frozen tableau as, his breath rasping in his throat, he slowly, but graciously, began to collapse, his eyes remaining wide and disbelieving on Toby as he did so.

As he stared at the little boy who was unmistakeably his grandson…

CHAPTER FOUR

'DO NOT speak! Not one word!' Gabriel warned harshly as he paced the hallway where he and Bella waited to hear news of his father.

Gabriel had managed to halt his father's collapse before he hit the floor. Bella had reminded Gabriel that her father was a doctor before rushing off to get him as Gabriel helped Cristo from the room with as little fuss as was possible in the circumstances.

Even so several concerned wedding guests, including the bride and groom, had followed them to hover outside the doorway of the small unoccupied room Gabriel had found to take his father to further down the hallway.

Henry Scott, Bella's father, had dealt firmly with those onlookers when he joined them a couple of minutes later, by ordering those guests back to the wedding reception and Gabriel and Bella out into the hallway while he examined his patient.

At last giving Gabriel the opportunity to deal with, to think of, the reason for his father's collapse!

That small boy—Bella's son—

His son, too…?

Bella flinched as Gabriel stopped his pacing to look down at her with dark, accusing eyes, knowing it would do no good now to deny what had been so patently obvious to Cristo Danti that he had collapsed from the shock of suddenly being confronted by his grandson.

She drew in a ragged breath. 'His name is Toby. Tobias,' she enlarged shakily. 'He's four years old.'

Gabriel's hands clenched into fists at his side. 'Four years and four months to be exact!'

Bella swallowed hard. 'Yes.'

Those dark eyes glittered menacingly. 'Where is he now?'

Bella straightened defensively. 'I took him back to sit with my mother and Liam. I— It frightened him when your father collapsed in that way.'

Gabriel looked at her coldly. 'Shock is apt to do that to a man who has already suffered three minor heart attacks in the last four years!'

Bella hadn't known that about Cristo Danti. Not that it would have made a lot of difference if she had known. Neither Gabriel nor his father were part of her own or Toby's lives.

At least, they hadn't been until now…

Gabriel, she had no doubt, wanted—no, he would demand—some answers from her concerning that. Just as the look on her own father's face, as he had looked first at Cristo Danti and then Gabriel, had told Bella he would no doubt like some answers, too, once he had finished examining his patient!

She gave a shaky sigh. 'I don't think this is the time or place to discuss this, Gabriel—'

'The time and place to discuss this would have been

almost five years ago when you first discovered you were pregnant!'

'As I recall you were no longer around to talk to almost five years ago!'

His mouth tightened. 'It was well publicised that I was in Italy at the time, at the Danti vineyards, recovering from the injuries I sustained in the car crash!'

Bella's eyes flashed deeply purple. 'And you seriously think that I was going to follow you there and tell you the news!'

'You had no right to keep my son's existence from me!' A nerve pulsed in Gabriel's tightly clenched jaw.

She shook her head. 'You gave up any right you had to know about Toby by the fact that you never phoned me as you promised and only slept with me that night out of jealousy and spite because of your ex-girlfriend's relationship with Paulo Descari!'

Gabriel's face darkened dangerously. 'I—'

'Could the two of you please save your—*discussion*—until later?' Henry Scott had opened the door of the room where Gabriel could see his father lying back on one of the sofas. 'I think your father has merely suffered a severe shock rather than another heart attack, Mr Danti, but to be on the safe side I would like to get him to a hospital for a check-up.'

'Daddy…?' Bella looked across at her father uncertainly.

He gave her a reassuring smile. 'It's okay, Bella,' he said gently. 'For the moment let's just concentrate on getting Mr Danti to hospital, hmm?'

Bella didn't need to be told any plainer that her father had guessed Toby's relationship to the two Danti men.

What must her father think of her?

More to the point, what must he think of the fact that Gabriel Danti, of all men, was unmistakeably the father of his grandson?

'I would like to see my son.'

Bella had remained behind at the hotel to put Toby to bed when Gabriel and her father had accompanied Cristo Danti to the hospital. But she hadn't made any attempt to go to bed herself. Had known—had been absolutely certain, in fact—that Gabriel would return once he had assured himself of his father's recovery.

It was almost two o'clock in the morning, but nevertheless Bella had been expecting the knock on the door of the sitting-room between the bedroom she shared with Claudia and the one Liam shared with Toby. She had changed out of the dress she had worn to the wedding, and into fitted jeans and a black T-shirt, in anticipation of this meeting.

Gabriel looked grim, to say the least, that scar down his left cheek more noticeable in his harshly set features, his eyes fierce as he looked down at her challengingly.

Bella opened the door wider so that Gabriel could step inside the suite. 'Toby is asleep,' she told him calmly as she closed the door behind him before turning to face him.

That scar on Gabriel's cheek seemed to pulse as he clenched his jaw tightly. 'Nevertheless, I wish to see him.'

'How is your father?'

'Tests have shown your father's original diagnosis to be the correct one. It was shock that caused my father's collapse and not a heart attack. He is to remain in hospital overnight for observation, but they expect to discharge him in the morning. Isabella—'

'Did my father return with you from the hospital?' Bella had already had one long, uncomfortable conversation with her mother this evening, she wasn't sure she would be up to another one with her father once Gabriel had left.

Gabriel gave a terse nod. 'He told me to tell you he will speak with you in the morning.'

Her eyes widened. 'He knew you were coming here?' Even as she asked the question Bella knew the answer; how else would Gabriel have known which suite to come to in order to see her if her father hadn't told him?

Gabriel's mouth thinned. 'He realised I would want to see my son again before I left, yes.'

Bella flinched every time he said that. No matter what his biological make-up might be, Toby was her son, not Gabriel's.

She gave a firm shake of her head. 'I don't think that's a good idea—'

Gabriel's scornful laugh cut across her refusal. 'Any concern I might have felt for your wishes died the moment I discovered you had kept my son's existence from me for over four years!' He made no effort to hide his contempt.

He had a son!

Gabriel still found it incredible that such a person existed. That there was a small, tousle-haired boy in the adjoining bedroom with his dark curls and eyes, and a small dimple in the centre of his still-babyish chin…

Having been denied all knowledge of him for over

four years, Gabriel had no intention of letting that continue a minute—even a second—longer!

'Where is he, Isabella?' he rasped furiously, her panicked glance towards the door to the right of the room enough for Gabriel to stride towards it determinedly.

'Where are you going?'

Gabriel ignored Bella's protest as he gently pushed that door open, recognising the sleeping boy in the first bed as Liam Scott before he turned his attention to the much smaller child in the second bed.

His breath caught in his throat as he looked down at the little boy he now knew to be his own son. Toby. Tobias.

He was beautiful, Gabriel acknowledged achingly. Absolutely beautiful. A perfect combination of his two parents.

Toby had Gabriel's hair colour and that dimple on his chin that would one day become a cleft exactly like those of his father and grandfather. The smoothness of Toby's brow and the long lashes that swept his cheeks were his mother's, as was that perfect bow of a mouth with its fuller top lip.

His!

This beautiful child was of his loins. Of his blood.

Bella could only stand helplessly by as Gabriel dropped to his knees beside Toby's bed, her protest strangling in her throat as Gabriel reached out a hand to touch the little boy, the stroke of his fingers against one slightly chubby cheek so gentle, so tender, that Toby didn't even stir.

Her heart felt as if it were breaking, shattering, as she watched the rush of love that softened Gabriel's harshly hewn features. As she saw that love glowing in his broodingly dark gaze as he continued to stare at his son in wonder.

And she knew without a doubt that the last four years of sharing Toby only with her family were over…

'I need a drink,' Gabriel stated flatly some time later when he had reluctantly left his son's bedside to return to the sitting-room, not waiting for Bella's reply but moving to the mini-bar to help himself to one of the small bottles of whisky before pouring it into a glass and drinking most of it in one swallow. 'So, Isabella,' he stated as he looked across at her grimly. 'What do you suggest we do about this situation?'

'What situation?' she repeated sharply, her stance wholly defensive as she stood across the room.

Gabriel looked at her through narrowed lids. He had made love with this woman a little over five years ago. That lovemaking had resulted in a child. A child whose existence she had deliberately kept from him. For that alone Isabella deserved no mercy from him.

His mouth thinned. 'The situation that Toby, despite what you may have decided to the contrary, deserves to know both of his parents rather than just one!'

Her throat moved convulsively, but otherwise she maintained her defensive stance. 'As I have already explained—'

'As far as you are concerned, I gave up the right to know my own child because *you* believe I only went to bed with you out of jealousy and spite over my ex-girl-friend's relationship with Paulo Descari,' Gabriel coldly repeated her earlier accusation. 'Neither jealousy nor spite were part of my emotions that night, Isabella,' he added curtly. 'And I certainly wasn't feeling those emotions at the time of the accident the following day either,' he bit out deliberately.

Bella moistened lips that had gone suddenly dry as she sensed the leashed violence in him. 'I didn't suggest they were, Gabriel. You did.'

He gave a scathing snort. 'It is impossible not to do so considering Janine's claims following the accident,' Gabriel snarled. 'The official enquiry proved my innocence in the matter. But perhaps you would prefer to believe that I am responsible for the accident that caused the death of two other men, rather than take my word for what happened that day?'

Bella felt the colour drain from her cheeks even as she stared at Gabriel. No, of course she didn't prefer to believe that Gabriel had deliberately caused the accident that had killed two other men. She didn't believe it!

Gabriel might be guilty of many things, but Bella certainly hadn't ever believed him to be guilty of that.

Gabriel looked at her coldly. 'I did *not* cause the accident, Isabella,' he repeated firmly. 'That was only the hysterical accusation of a woman who took advantage of the fact that I was unconscious for several days following the crash, and so was unable to deny those accusations.'

And that accusation hadn't been the reason Bella had made no effort to contact Gabriel following the car crash, either…

How could she possibly have just arrived at the hospital and asked to be allowed to see Gabriel when they had only spent a single night together?

If Gabriel wanted to see her again, Bella had reasoned, then he would contact her just as he'd said he would. Until he chose to do that—if he chose to do that!—she would just have to get on with her life as best she could.

Her pregnancy had been something Bella simply hadn't taken into account when she had made that decision.

Weeks later, after her pregnancy was confirmed, Bella had been forced to make choices, both for herself and her baby. Gabriel's failure to phone had simply re-inforced Bella's suspicion that he would want nothing to do with them. Or if he did, he had the power to take her baby away from her. Something Bella would never allow to happen. It was too late now, far too late, for her to explain or undo any of those choices…

Gabriel watched the emotions that flickered across Bella's beautiful and expressive face, too fleeting for him to be able to discern any of them accurately. 'I did not cause the accident, Isabella, but that does not mean I have not carried the guilt of Paulo and Jason's deaths with me every day since.'

'But why?' She looked totally confused now.

Gabriel turned away to look out of the window at the San Francisco skyline.

How could he ever explain to her how he had felt five years ago when he'd regained consciousness and learnt of Paulo Descari and Jason Miller's deaths? Of Janine's hysterical accusations?

Added to that, Gabriel had felt utter despair, even helplessness, at the seriousness of his own injuries.

The cuts and burns to his body that were still visible, five years later, in the scar on his face and those that laced across his chest, back, and legs. The crushing of his pelvis and legs had kept him confined to bed for months, with the added possibility that he might never walk again.

Worst of all, worse even than Paulo and Jason's deaths, Janine's duplicity, had been the knowledge that their night together had meant so little to Bella that—

No!

Gabriel refused to go there. He had not thought of Bella's desertion for almost five years. He would not—could not—think of it now.

Now he would think only of Toby. Of his *son*. And Bella's second betrayal…

He turned back to face Bella, his expression utterly implacable. 'Toby is all that is important now,' Gabriel told her icily. 'I will return at ten o'clock tomorrow—or rather, today,' he corrected, 'at which time you and Toby will be ready to accompany me—'

'I'm not going anywhere with you, Gabriel, and neither is Toby,' Bella cut in immediately.

'At which time,' he repeated in, if possible, even icier tones, 'you and Toby will be ready to accompany me on a visit to my father. Toby's grandfather,' he added harshly.

Bella's second denial died unspoken on her lips.

She had talked with her mother earlier tonight. Or rather, her mother had talked with her. A conversation in which her mother had assured Bella that the relationship between herself and Gabriel was their own affair, and for the two of them alone to unravel. However, speaking as a grandmother, she had added, she had nothing but sympathy for Cristo Danti and the fact that he had only learnt this evening of his grandson's existence. That knowledge had been obviously so emotionally profound it had resulted in the older man's collapse.

An irrefutable fact against which Bella had no defence. Either earlier or now.

Her shoulders were stiff with tension. 'Firstly, let me tell you that I deeply resent your use of emotional blackmail in order to get me to do what you want—'

'Would you rather I pursued a legal claim, instead?' Gabriel challenged contemptuously.

Bella swallowed hard even as she refused to lower her gaze from his. 'That would take months, by which time I would be safely back in England.'

'I will have my lawyers apply for an immediate injunction to prevent you, or Toby, from leaving this country,' Gabriel warned scathingly. 'I am a Danti, Isabella,' he reminded her.

Her eyes flashed darkly purple at his underlying threat. 'Secondly,' she pointedly resumed her earlier conversation, 'despite the fact that I resent your methods, I am nevertheless perfectly aware of your father's claim as Toby's grandfather—'

'But not my own as his father!' Gabriel was so furiously angry now that there was a white line about the firmness of his mouth and his body was rigid with suppressed emotion.

Bella looked at him sadly, knowing this conversation was achieving nothing except to drive a distance between the two of them that was even wider than the gaping chasm that already existed.

She had known when she met Gabriel again yesterday that he wasn't the same man she had been so attracted to five years ago that she had forgotten, or simply put aside, every vestige of caution in order to spend the night in his arms.

This Gabriel was scarred on the inside as well as the outside and the coldness of his anger concerning her having kept Toby's existence a secret from him was worse than any emotional accusations might have been.

She sighed. 'Ten o'clock, I believe you said?'

Gabriel's eyes narrowed on her, searching for any sign of deception in her eyes or expression. He could see none. Only a weary acceptance of a situation she could do nothing to change.

The tension in his shoulders relaxed slightly. 'We will sit down together with Toby first and explain my own and my father's relationship to him.'

'Isn't that a little premature?' Bella protested.

'In my opinion it is almost four and a half years too late!' Gabriel snapped.

'It will only confuse Toby when you have no active role in his life—'

His scornful laugh cut off her protest. 'Do you *seriously* believe that is going to continue?'

Bella looked at him, knowing by the implacability in Gabriel's expression as he looked down the length of his arrogant nose at her—the same implacability in his tone whenever he now referred to her as *Isabella*—that it wasn't. That it was Gabriel's intention to take an extremely active role in Toby's life in future.

Precisely where that left her, Bella had no idea…

CHAPTER FIVE

'DOES Grandad live in one of these big houses?'

'He certainly does, Toby,' Gabriel answered him indulgently.

Bella would never cease to be amazed by the resilience of children and by her own child's in particular.

Having lain awake long into the night dreading, planning, how best to break the news to Toby that Gabriel Danti was his father and Cristo Danti was his grandfather, she had been totally surprised by Toby taking the whole thing in his four-year-old stride.

Even his initial shyness at suddenly being presented with a father had quickly given way to excitement as he was strapped into the back of Gabriel's open-topped sports car to make the drive over to the house where his grandfather was anxiously waiting to meet him after being discharged from the hospital earlier this morning.

Bella's own emotions were far less simplistic as she stared out of the car window, seeing none of the beauty of the Pacific Ocean in the distance, her thoughts all inwards.

Her life, and consequently Toby's, was back in

England. In the small village where she had bought a cottage for the two of them to live in, once she had been financially able to do so, after living with her parents for the first two years of Toby's life. She liked living in a village, as did Toby, and he was due to start attending the local school in September.

This situation with Gabriel, his veiled threats of the night before, made Bella wonder exactly when she could expect to return to that life.

Not that she was able to read any of Gabriel's thoughts or feelings this morning. He was wearing sunglasses now, and his mood when he had arrived at the hotel earlier had been necessarily upbeat for Toby's benefit, his attitude towards Bella one of strained politeness. Only the coldness in Gabriel's eyes earlier, whenever he had chanced to look at her, had told Bella of the anger he still felt towards her.

The anger he would probably always feel towards her for denying him knowledge of his son for the first four years of Toby's life…

'Here we are, Toby,' Gabriel turned to tell his son after steering the car into the driveway, smiling as he saw the excitement on his son's face as they waited for the electrically operated gates to open so that he could drive them down to the house.

His son…!

Even twelve hours later Gabriel still had trouble believing he had a son. A bright, happy, and unaffected little boy who had taken the news of Gabriel being his father much more pragmatically than Gabriel had responded the evening before to learning that he had a son.

Gabriel glanced at Bella now from behind his dark sunglasses, his mouth thinning as he noted the pallor to her cheeks, the lines of strain beside her eyes and mouth.

Deservedly so!

Whatever claims Janine Childe had made against him five years ago did not change the fact that Bella hadn't so much as attempted to inform him she was expecting his child, that she had actually borne him a son, or that she had then brought Toby up with no knowledge whatsoever of his father or his father's family.

'Your own family are all aware now of Toby's paternity?'

Bella was glad she was wearing sunglasses to hide the sudden tears that had welled up in her eyes at the emotional breakfast she had shared earlier with her parents and siblings.

There had been no words of rebuke or disapproval from her parents, only their gentle understanding as she explained the situation of five years ago to them— and Claudia's demand, as the two sisters had returned to their hotel suite once the meal was over, that Bella 'tell all' about the night she had spent in Gabriel's bed. A curiosity Bella had chosen not to satisfy.

She didn't even want to think about that night, let alone relive, even verbally, how completely she had been infatuated with the darkly seductive Gabriel Danti five years ago!

'Yes,' she confirmed huskily.

Gabriel nodded in satisfaction as he accelerated the black sports car down the driveway to the house that was just as grand as Bella would have expected of this prestigious area of San Francisco. It was large and gabled, slightly Victorian in style, with its redbrick structure and the white frames to the stained-glass windows.

'You're sure this…visit…isn't going to give your father a relapse?' Bella hung back reluctantly on the gravelled driveway once they were all out of the car.

Gabriel had removed his sunglasses and left them in the car, his expression mocking as he glanced down at her. 'On the contrary, I believe its possibilities will achieve the opposite.'

Bella looked up at him, a little confused by the cryptic comment. 'Sorry?'

His mouth tightened. 'Later, Isabella,' he said curtly. 'You and I are going to talk again later.'

Bella didn't much like the sound of that.

And she was really starting to dislike the way Gabriel kept calling her *Isabella* in that coldly contemptuous way!

Once Gabriel had left the previous night Bella had thought long and hard about his claim that he hadn't made love with her five years ago, or spent the night with her, in an effort to make Janine Childe jealous. After hours and hours of going over the situation in her head, Bella had finally come to the conclusion that it really didn't matter what Gabriel's reasons had been.

They had spent only that single night together. Admittedly it had been an intensely passionate, even erotic night, but nevertheless that was all it had been. On Gabriel's side, anyway. That Bella had experienced strong feelings for him after that night didn't change the fact that Gabriel hadn't felt that way about her.

As the last five years of silence on Gabriel's part showed…

He had never made any attempt to contact her again after that night although that had been his promise. Admittedly Gabriel had been involved in the car crash later that day, but he hadn't suffered memory loss. Once he had recovered enough to be able to talk, to receive visitors, that needn't have stopped him from getting in touch. Not too much to ask if Gabriel really had been interested in seeing her again. Which he obviously hadn't… That was not the kind of man she wanted as a father for her child!

She shook her head. 'I don't think we have anything left to talk about, Gabriel,' she told him firmly.

Gabriel gave a brief, humourless smile. 'We have not even begun to talk yet, Isabella!'

His father was waiting for them in the warmth of the plant-filled conservatory at the back of the house, Gabriel appreciating that the informality of such surroundings was exactly what was needed to put a four-year-old boy at his ease.

That his father found the meeting highly emotional Gabriel had no doubts, Cristo's voice husky with suppressed tears as Toby joined him and he allowed the little boy to water the orchids for him.

'I am neglecting your mother, Toby,' Cristo apologised some minutes later as he straightened. 'You may continue to water if you wish, Toby, or you may come and sit with us while your mother and I talk.'

Bella knew exactly which choice her young son would make; like most small boys, Toby had absolutely no interest in the conversation of adults!

'Bella.' Cristo Danti's voice was deep with emotion as he crossed the room to where she had sat in one of the half a dozen cane chairs watching him and Toby together. He took her hand in his to raise it to his lips as she stood up. 'Thank you for bringing Toby to see me,' he told her, his eyes slightly moist as he looked at her.

Bella felt her own tears clogging her throat as she looked at Gabriel's father, not able to discern any reproach in the directness of that brown gaze, only the slight sheen of the tears that he made no effort to hide from her.

Bella was very aware of the menacingly silent Gabriel standing beside her. 'I—' she moistened her lips nervously '—I really don't know what to say,' she stuttered, aware that statement was painfully inadequate and yet totally true.

'Gabriel has already explained all that needs to be explained.' Cristo Danti smiled at her reassuringly. 'All that really matters is that you and Toby are here now.'

Bella, besides feeling the heavy weight of guilt at Cristo Danti's complete acceptance of a situation that yesterday evening had caused his collapse, also wondered exactly what Gabriel had explained…

'You're very kind,' she told the older man as she squeezed his hand before releasing it.

'Obviously Isabella and I have much to talk about yet, Papa,' Gabriel spoke abruptly beside her. 'If you and Toby will excuse us for a few minutes…?'

Bella felt a sense of rising panic at the suggestion, not sure she was up to another confrontation with Gabriel at the moment. She hadn't slept much during what had been left of the previous night, and the morning had already been traumatic enough with the conversation with her family, followed by Gabriel's arrival at the hotel and their explanation to Toby, and now this meeting with Cristo Danti.

But a single glance at the grim determination of Gabriel's set expression was enough to tell Bella that she didn't have any choice in the matter!

'Toby...?' she prompted lightly to gain her young son's attention from watering the plants. 'Will you be okay while I just go and have a little chat with—with—your father?' That didn't get any easier with actually saying out loud!

'Of course.' Toby beamed across at her unconcernedly.

Bella wished at that moment that her young son weren't quite so gregarious; obviously she wasn't going to get any help at all from Toby in avoiding another confrontation with Gabriel.

To Toby, Bella knew, this was obviously all just a big adventure; he had absolutely no idea of the underlying tensions—or the possible repercussions!—of Gabriel Danti being his father and Cristo Danti being his grandfather.

Bella wanted to make sure it remained that way...

'I am sure Toby and I will be able to keep each other amused, Bella,' Cristo assured her.

She gave him a grateful smile, that smile fading as Gabriel stood back politely to allow her to precede him into the main house. Polite, even coldly polite, Bella could deal with—she just didn't think that politeness was going to last for very long once she and Gabriel were alone together!

'He'll probably drown your poor father's orchids for

him,' Bella murmured ruefully as Gabriel moved ahead to open a door further down the hallway.

Gabriel glanced back at her, his gaze hooded. 'I doubt my father will mind, do you?' he said pointedly as he pushed open the door to the room before standing back to allow her to enter.

It was a book-lined room, Bella noted with dismay, much like the study in the Danti's English home in Surrey where she and Gabriel had first met.

Gabriel was also aware of the irony of their surroundings as he quietly closed the door behind them before moving to sit behind the green leather-topped desk, his gaze narrowed on Bella as she chose not to sit in the chair facing that desk—and him!—but instead moved to look out of the huge picture-window, her back firmly turned towards him.

She had pulled her hair back today and secured it up in a loose knot at her crown, her exposed neck appearing fragile in its slenderness, her shoulders narrow beneath the soft material of the cream blouse she wore with black fitted trousers.

She appeared slight, even delicate, but Gabriel knew that appearance to be deceptive—Isabella Scott was more than capable of defending both herself and Toby if the need should arise. In Toby's case, as far as Gabriel was concerned, it didn't. Bella herself was a different matter, however…

His mouth firmed in exasperation. 'Ignoring me will not make me go away, Isabella!'

She turned, her smile rueful. 'If only!'

Gabriel regarded her coldly. 'You have had things completely your own way for the last five years—'

'What *things*?' she came back tartly, her body tense. 'I was twenty-one years old at the time, Gabriel. Only twenty-one!' she emphasised. 'Having a baby wasn't in my immediate plans back then, let alone one whose father wasn't even living in the same country as me when that baby was born!'

'It does no good to get angry, Isabella—'

'It does *me* good, Gabriel!' she contradicted him vehemently. 'You have made it clear you disapprove of my actions five years ago, so I'm just trying to explain to you that I did what I thought was best—'

'For whom?' Gabriel sat back in his chair to look at her intently.

'For everyone!'

Gabriel's jaw clenched. 'In what way was it *best* for Toby that he was not even aware of his father or his father's family? In what way was it *best* for him that he did not have the comforts that being a Danti could have given him—?'

'Toby hasn't gone without a single thing—'

'He has gone without a *father*!' Gabriel's voice was icy cold, his accusation indisputable.

Bella drew in a controlling breath, very aware that letting this conversation dissolve into another slanging match would settle none of the things that stood between herself and Gabriel. The main one, of course, being Toby…

She shook her head. 'I assure you that my own parents have been wonderful,' she told him huskily. 'Claudia and Liam, too. And once I was able to work I made sure that Toby wanted for nothing.'

'At what did you work?' Gabriel asked.

Bella gave a grimace. 'I was completely at a loss as to what job I could do once I discovered I was pregnant. But I had written my thesis at university on the life of Leonardo da Vinci. My tutor thought it might be good enough for publishing, so during the months of my pregnancy I approached a publishing company to see if they were interested. With a lot more hard work, and another fifty thousand words, they accepted it. I was fortunate in that its publication coincided with a fiction book on a similar theme that was very popular at the time.' She gave a rueful shrug. 'I've had two books at the top of the non-fiction bestseller list in the last three years,' she added quietly.

Gabriel realised now where Bella's self-assurance and that air of quiet self-containment came from. In spite of her unexpected pregnancy, and the difficulty involved with being a single mother, Bella had still managed to achieve success in her chosen career.

'That is—commendable.'

Bella gave a tight smile. 'But unexpected?'

Gabriel couldn't deny that Bella's obvious financial independence was something he hadn't taken into consideration when contemplating a solution to their present problem.

Although perhaps he should have done?

Her suite at the hotel would have been costly, and Bella's clothes were obviously designer-label, as were the T-shirt and shorts Toby was wearing today.

'Perhaps,' he allowed after a pause. 'But ultimately it changes nothing,' he pointed out.

Bella gave a puzzled frown. 'I'm sorry...I don't understand?'

'Toby is *my* son—'

'I believe I've already acknowledged that fact,' she snapped.

Gabriel eyed her mockingly. 'Undeniable, is it not?' he murmured with satisfaction, Toby's likeness to both himself and his father so obvious it had caused his father to collapse with the shock of it. Gabriel's mouth tightened. 'The only solution open to us is that we will be married as soon as I am able to make the arrangements—'

'No!' Bella protested forcefully, her expression one of horror. 'No, Gabriel,' she repeated determinedly, her chin once again raised in the familiar air of challenge. 'I have no intention of marrying you, either now or in the future.'

Bella was absolutely astounded that Gabriel should have suggested marriage to her. Suggested it? Gabriel hadn't *suggested* anything—he had stated it as a foregone conclusion!

Five years ago Bella had considered all of the options, despite the complication of Gabriel's feelings for Janine Childe, if she were to go to Gabriel and tell him of her pregnancy.

The offer of his financial help was obviously one of them, and Bella had rejected that on principle; no matter how hard a struggle it might be for her to manage on her own, she did not want to be beholden to Gabriel Danti in that way.

That he might want to marry her, for the sake of the baby, had been a less likely option considering they had only had a one-night stand, and one that Bella had rejected even more vehemently than she had the idea of Gabriel's financial help.

She didn't want to marry anyone just because they had made a child together.

'Do you not want to marry me because you lied when you said you are not repulsed by my scars?' Gabriel rasped harshly, his eyes narrowed to dangerous slits, a nerve pulsing in his tightly clenched jaw.

Bella shook her head. 'I'm not in the least repulsed by them,' she insisted quietly.

His gaze was glacial. 'Most women would be.'

'Well I'm not "most women",' Bella said, furiously. 'Gabriel, acknowledge Toby as your son, by all means, but please leave me out of the equation,' she pleaded.

Gabriel's mouth twisted. 'That might be a little difficult when you are Toby's mother.'

She shook her head. 'I'm sure we can work out some sort of visiting—' She broke off as Gabriel stood up abruptly.

'Is that what you want for Toby?' he asked harshly, the scar on his cheek seeming to stand out more severely. 'You want him to become nothing more than a human parcel that passes between the two of us?'

'It doesn't have to be like that,' she protested emotionally.

'If the two of us do not marry that is exactly what it will be like,' Gabriel insisted impatiently.

Bella swallowed hard, her expression pained. 'You think Toby will fare any better as the only lynchpin between two people who don't love each other but are married to each other?'

'You have said you do not find my more obvious scars—unacceptable.' Gabriel moved close enough now to see the slight flush that slowly crept into her cheeks, and the rapid rise and fall of her breasts beneath the cream blouse.

'I don't.' She frowned. 'But that doesn't mean I like the idea of marrying you!'

Bella couldn't think straight when Gabriel was standing so close to her. Couldn't concentrate on anything with the heat of his dark gaze moving slowly over her body to linger on the firm thrust of her breasts, breasts that responded in tingling awareness, the nipples suddenly hard against the soft material of her bra and blouse. A warm, aching surge between her thighs made her shift uncomfortably.

She moistened lips that had gone suddenly dry. 'Physical attraction is not a basis for marriage, either.' Even as she said the words Bella was aware that her denial lacked any force.

'Surely you will agree it is a start?' Gabriel murmured huskily, a look of deep satisfaction in his eyes.

She could barely breathe as Gabriel easily held her gaze with his, allowing her to see the warmth burning deep within those dark brown eyes. Then he stepped close enough for her to be aware of the hard press of his arousal against her and his head lowered with the obvious intention of claiming her mouth with his own…

It was like a dam bursting as their mouths fused hotly together. Bella's fingers became entangled in the dark thickness of Gabriel's hair as their bodies pressed demandingly against each other. Their kiss deepened fiercely, spiralling out of control when Gabriel's tongue moved to duel with hers as he enticed her to claim him as he was claiming her.

Bella was so hungry for this. The aching emptiness

inside her was completely filled when Gabriel pushed
the soft material of her blouse aside to cup and hold her
breast, the soft pad of his thumb moving urgently, arous-
ingly, over the hardened nub.

Bella almost ripped Gabriel's shirt undone as she satisfied her own need to touch his naked flesh. The hard
ripple of muscle. The dark silkiness of the hair that
covered his chest. Fingers tracing the fine lines of the
scars he still bore from his accident five years ago,
Gabriel responding to those caresses with a low groan
in his throat.

She offered no resistance as Gabriel snapped the
back fastening to her bra to release her breasts to his
questing hands, her throat arching, breath gasping as
Gabriel's lips parted from hers to draw one hardened
nipple into the hot, moist cavern of his mouth, and his
tongue flickered and rasped over that sensitive nub as
his hand cupped and caressed her other breast.

The ache between Bella's thighs became hot and
damp, an aching void needing to be filled as she felt the
hardness of Gabriel's arousal, rubbing herself against
him as the hardness of his thighs pulsed with the same
need. She offered no resistance when Gabriel's hands
moved to cup her bottom and he lifted her so that she
was sitting on the front of the desk, parting her legs so
that he could move inside them, his hardness now
centred on the throbbing nub that nestled there.

Bella groaned with satisfaction as Gabriel lay her
back on the desktop so that he could suckle the nakedness of her breasts with the same heated rhythm as his
erection thrust against the hardened nub between her
thighs. Bella's breathing became shallow, a husky rasp,

as her release began to burn, to explode, taking her over the edge of reason—

A soft knock on the study door sounded before Cristo Danti informed them, 'Toby and I will be outside in the garden when you have finished talking.'

Gabriel had moved sharply away from Bella the moment the knock sounded on the door, his mouth tightening now as he saw Bella's horrified expression before she pushed up from the desk and moved away from him to turn her back and rearrange her clothes. 'Isabella and I will join you shortly,' he answered his father distractedly as he pulled his shirt together.

'There is no rush,' his father assured pleasantly before he could be heard walking back down the hallway.

Gabriel frowned at Bella's back as she tried, and failed, to refasten her bra with fingers that were obviously shaking too badly to complete the task. 'Here, let me,' he rasped before moving to snap the hook back into place.

'Thank you,' she said stiffly, making no effort to turn as she quickly buttoned her blouse. 'I—I don't know what to say! That was— I'm not sure what happened…'

'Oh, I think you are well aware of what almost happened, Bella,' he drawled. 'It pleases me that you did not lie concerning my scars,' he added huskily.

Bella hadn't lied about Gabriel's physical scars; his inner ones were another matter, however…

She shook her head. 'I don't usually behave in that— in that way!'

'It is perhaps some time since you last had a man,' Gabriel pointed out dryly.

Bella turned sharply, a frown between her eyes as she

glared at him. Exactly what sort of woman did Gabriel think she was?

The sort of woman who allowed herself to almost be made love to on a desktop, apparently!

The sort of woman who had almost ripped Gabriel's shirt from his back in her need to touch his naked flesh!

Bella closed her eyes in self-disgust as she tried to reassemble her thoughts. She most certainly was *not* that sort of woman! Gabriel probably wouldn't believe her even if she were to tell him—which she had no intention of doing; it was bad enough that she knew how out of character her response to Gabriel had been without him knowing it, too!—that there hadn't been a man in her life on an intimate level since that single night she had spent with Gabriel five years ago.

How could there have been? For nine months of that time she had been pregnant with Toby. And since Toby's birth Bella had centred all of her attention on him. She certainly hadn't wanted to add any more confusion to his young life by giving him a succession of 'uncles'!

She drew in a deep controlling breath before opening her eyes to glare at Gabriel. He had pulled his shirt back onto his shoulders, but hadn't bothered to refasten it, and Bella could now see the fine pattern of scars that marred the smoothness of the olive-coloured skin. With his dark hair in disarray from her recently entangled fingers, and that unbuttoned shirt revealing his scarred chest, Gabriel looked more piratical than ever. Certainly more rakishly attractive than Bella felt comfortable with!

She raised dark, mocking brows. 'I'm sure it's been much longer for me than the last time you "had" a woman!'

Gabriel continued to look at her levelly for several tense seconds, and then a humourless smile curved those sculptured lips. 'Not all women are as—understanding, about physical imperfection, as you appear to be,' he said dryly.

Bella couldn't believe that. If Gabriel were any more perfect she would be a gibbering wreck!

'I believe that what took place just now proved that we would not lack physical gratification in our marriage,' he commented wickedly.

Bella's mouth tightened. 'We are *not* getting married,' she repeated firmly.

Gabriel looked unconcerned by her vehemence. 'Oh, I think that we are.'

'Really?' She frowned her uncertainty, not liking the assurance in Gabriel's tone at all.

Any more than she liked the smile that he now gave her. 'Really,' he drawled confidently. 'I am sure you must be aware of the benefits to you in such a marriage—'

'If you're referring to what happened between us just now, then forget it!' Bella glared at him. 'I can find that sort of "benefit" with any number of men!'

Gabriel's mouth compressed. 'There will be no other men in your life once we are married, Isabella. Now I am assured of your response, we will be married in the fullest sense of the word. As an only child myself, I am hoping it will be a marriage that will result in us having more children together. Lots of brothers and sisters for Toby.'

Bella was thrown momentarily off balance by that last claim as she easily imagined having more sons and daughters that looked exactly like Gabriel.

She gave a fierce shake of her head. 'You can't seriously want to spend the rest of your life married to a woman who doesn't love you—'

'Any more than you would wish to be married to a man who does not love you,' he acknowledged curtly. 'But the alternative is even less palatable. A long—and no doubt very public—legal battle for custody of Toby,' Gabriel said grimly.

Bella gasped as her greatest fear was made a possibility. 'You would do that to Toby?'

Gabriel gave a shrug. 'If you leave me with no other choice, yes.'

Bella looked at him searchingly, knowing by the utter implacability of Gabriel's expression that he meant every word he had just said. Marriage to him, or Gabriel would involve them all in a very messy legal battle.

She breathed in deeply. 'All right, Gabriel, I'll think about marrying you—'

'Thinking about it is not enough, Isabella,' he cut in harshly. 'Especially,' he added more softly, that dark gaze narrowed on her speculatively, 'when I suspect you are only delaying the inevitable in order that you and Toby might return to England tomorrow, as originally planned, with your family, yes?'

That was exactly the reason Bella was delaying giving Gabriel a definite answer!

She chewed on her bottom lip. 'I don't believe it's inevitable that the two of us will marry—'

'I beg to differ, Isabella.'

Her eyes flashed deeply purple. 'You've never begged in the whole of your privileged life!'

He lifted an autocratic eyebrow. 'And I am not about

to do so now, either,' he said. 'I want your answer before you leave here today.'

'You'll have my answer when I'm damned well ready to give it!' she flashed back heatedly.

Although Bella already had a feeling she knew what that answer was going to be.

What it *had* to be…

CHAPTER SIX

'WILL I see you in the morning, Daddy?'

Bella's breath caught in her throat as she waited for Gabriel to answer Toby. She was standing at the bottom of her son's bed watching the two of them as Toby lay tucked snugly beneath the duvet, Gabriel sitting at his side.

She had absolutely no doubts that Toby had enjoyed his day with his father and grandfather. The three of them had spent most of the morning out in the garden, Gabriel keeping Toby occupied with a number of ball games while Bella sat on a lounger watching them, dark sunglasses perched on the end of her nose as she allowed her thoughts to wander. The problem was, they kept coming back to the same place—Gabriel's insistence that she marry him…

As the day had progressed—a drive out to look at the Danti vineyard, and lunch eaten outside on the terrace at the magnificent villa there, and then dinner later that evening at a wonderful fish restaurant at Pier 39—it was impossible for Bella to deny that Gabriel was wonderful with Toby.

That he already loved Toby with the same fierceness that Bella did...

And that Toby loved Gabriel right back!

Looking at the two of them sitting together now on Toby's bed, so alike with their dark curling hair and chocolate-brown eyes, and that cleft in the centre of their chins, Bella couldn't help feeling that she was fighting a losing battle. That even attempting to fight this harder, more arrogant Gabriel was a waste of her time and emotions.

Gabriel glanced down at her now, the expression in his eyes unreadable. 'I think that depends on Mummy, don't you?' he murmured.

'Mummy?' Toby prompted eagerly.

Bella drew in a ragged breath before answering. 'We'll see,' she finally said non-committally.

'That usually means yes,' Toby confided as he looked up at Gabriel conspiratorially.

'It does?' The darkness of Gabriel's gaze was mocking as he glanced across at Bella.

'It means we'll see,' she insisted. 'Now it's time for you to go to sleep, young man,' she told her son firmly as she moved to tuck him more comfortably beneath the covers. 'G—Daddy and I will just be in the other room if you should need us, Toby,' she added reassuringly before bending down to kiss him.

Toby reached up to wrap his arms about her neck as he hugged her. 'It was a lovely day, wasn't it, Mummy?'

Emotion caught in Bella's throat as she looked down into her son's happily beaming face.

Could she endanger that unclouded happiness by subjecting Toby to the trauma that a legal battle with

Gabriel was sure to cause? Could she really put Toby into a position where he would almost be forced to choose between the mother he had lived with all of his young life and the father he had only just met? Could she do that to him?

Surely the answer to all of those questions was no…

'Lovely,' she answered Toby brightly before kissing him again.

'I'll see you in the morning, darling.' She ruffled his dark curls before stepping away from the bed.

'We will both see you in the morning, Toby,' Gabriel added pointedly as he moved to receive Toby's hug goodnight.

Gabriel's arms were gentle, but his emotions were not. Toby, his son, now represented everything to him, the past, the present, and most definitely the future.

'Sleep now, little one,' he said huskily as he released Toby to step back.

'You promise you'll come back in the morning?' Toby's eyes were anxious.

Gabriel doubted that Toby heard the sob in his mother's throat as she stood just behind him, but Gabriel certainly did. 'I will come back in the morning,' he assured the little boy. Whatever it took, Gabriel was determined to be in Toby's life every morning!

'What would you have done about this situation if you had already been married to someone else when you learnt of Toby's existence?' Bella challenged once the two of them had returned to the sitting-room.

Gabriel's mouth tightened. 'Fortunately, that problem does not arise.'

'But if it had?' she insisted.

He shrugged. 'I refuse to answer a "what if" question, Isabella.'

She gave a little huff of frustration. 'Doesn't it bother you that I don't want to marry you?'

It should, and it did. But Gabriel knew from Bella's response to him earlier today that on one level, at least, she did want to be with him...

Other marriages, he was sure, had begun with less.

'Not particularly,' Gabriel dismissed curtly.

Bella continued to glare at him for several more seconds before she gave a sigh of defeat. 'All right, Gabriel, I will agree to marry you—'

'I thought that you would,' Gabriel murmured as he moved to sit in one of the armchairs.

'If you will allow me to finish...?' She raised dark, expressive brows as she stood across the room from him.

'By all means.' Gabriel relaxed back in the armchair. He had won the first battle—and the most difficult, he hoped—and so could now afford to be gracious in victory.

'Thank you,' she accepted dryly. 'I will agree to marry you,' she repeated, then went on more firmly, 'but only on certain conditions.'

Gabriel's gaze narrowed as he easily guessed, from the calmness of Bella's expression, that he wasn't going to like those conditions. 'Which are?'

'Firstly, if we married I would like to continue living in England—'

'I am sure that can be arranged.' He nodded, having already considered this problem earlier today when he had decided that marriage between himself and Isabella was the only real solution to Toby's continued welfare.

It would be a simple enough process to put a

manager in charge of the vineyards here, with the occasional visit from him to make sure they were being run properly.

'The Danti business interests are international, Isabella,' he informed her. 'I will simply take over the running of our London office. Your second condition…?'

'Toby will attend schools of my choice—'

'As long as that choice eventually includes Eton and then Cambridge, I do not foresee that as being a problem,' Gabriel drawled.

'Eton and Cambridge?' Bella echoed disbelievingly.

'The Dantis have been educated at Eton and Cambridge for several generations.'

Bella shook her head. 'Toby will begin attending the local school in September. Following that he will be a day-pupil at another local school.'

Gabriel quirked one dark brow. 'Then I suggest we ensure that we have already moved into a house close enough so that he can attend Eton school as a day-pupil.'

He looked so damned smug, Bella fumed inwardly. So sure of himself.

As he had no doubt been sure of what her answer to his marriage proposal would be. Proposal? Hah! Gabriel didn't ask, he ordered; he was arrogance personified!

But, while Toby had been enjoying himself as the centre of Cristo Danti and Gabriel's attention, Bella had spent most of the day considering her options. Her limited options, she had very quickly realised, considering there was no way now of denying that Toby was Gabriel's son—even if Bella did attempt to deny it, a simple blood test would prove her a liar!

Just as there was no denying that the Dantis were a very rich and powerful family, both here and in Europe. In reality, what possible chance did she have of ensuring that she and Toby—especially Toby!—came out of a legal battle unscathed? The answer to that was only too clear. Against Gabriel Danti she had no chance.

But if she was forced to agree to this marriage, then Bella was determined to have at least some say in what she would and would not agree to!

'Thirdly,' she snapped, 'the marriage will be in name only.' She looked across at him challengingly, her eyes widening in alarm as he suddenly stood up.

Gabriel slowly shook his head. 'I am sure that you are already well aware that will not be possible.'

Because of their response to each other earlier today!

A response that still made Bella cringe whenever she thought about it—which she had tried very hard not to do all day. She never responded to men in that totally wild and wanton way. At least…she never had until Gabriel. Both five years ago and then again today…

Which was why Bella was making this the last condition to their marriage. She could imagine nothing worse than becoming a slave to the desire that Gabriel seemed to ignite in her so easily.

Even now, feeling angry and trapped, Bella was still totally aware of Gabriel in the black shirt and faded jeans. Clearly remembered pushing that shirt from his shoulders earlier so that she might touch the warm, muscled flesh beneath it. Unfortunately, she remembered even more distinctly the way that Gabriel had touched her…

She would not, could not allow her emotions, her life, to be ruled by the desire Gabriel made her feel!

She straightened her shoulders. 'Without your agreement to that last condition I couldn't even contemplate the idea of the two of us marrying each other.'

Gabriel looked at her from under hooded lids, knowing by the steadiness of Bella's gaze, the sheer determination in her expression, that she thought she meant every word she was saying, at least. Considering their response to each other in his study earlier today, Gabriel found that very hard to believe. Or accept.

Bella had come alive in his arms. Wildly. Fiercely. Demandingly. How could she possibly imagine they could live together, day after day—night after night!—and not take that lovemaking to its inevitable conclusion?

His mouth tightened. 'You wish for Toby to be an only child?'

She shrugged. 'He was going to be that, anyway.'

Gabriel studied her closely. 'You are a beautiful woman, Isabella; if we had not met again you would no doubt have married one day and had other children.'

'No,' she answered flatly. 'I decided long ago that I would never subject Toby to a stepfather who may or may not have accepted him as his own,' she explained simply as Gabriel frowned at her.

The mere thought of Toby or Bella ever belonging to another man filled Gabriel with uncontrollable fury. Toby was his. Bella was his!

His hands clenched at his sides. 'I agree to your last condition, Bella—'

'I thought that you would,' she dryly echoed his earlier comment.

'Like you, Bella, I have not finished,' Gabriel replied.

'I agree to your last condition on the basis that it can be nullified, by you, at any time.'

Bella eyed him warily. 'What exactly does that mean?'

His smile was mocking. 'It means that I reserve the right to—*persuade* you, shall we say, into changing your mind.'

Bella had no doubt that what Gabriel meant by that remark was that he reserved the right to try and *seduce* her into changing her mind any time he felt like it!

Would she be able to resist him? Living with Gabriel twenty-four hours a day, every day, would she be able to withstand a Gabriel bent on seduction?

Did she have any real choice other than to try?

'You took me by surprise earlier, Gabriel,' she stated bravely. 'In future I will be on my guard against—well, against any attempt on your part to renew such attentions!'

She sounded so serious, so firm in her resolve, Gabriel acknowledged with a grudging admiration. 'I will allow no other men in your life, Isabella,' he warned her seriously.

'And will that rule apply to you, too?' she snapped.

Gabriel eyed her mockingly. 'My own tastes do not run in that particular direction—'

'You know very well what I meant!' She glared her exasperation.

He shrugged. 'There will be no other women in my bed but you, Isabella,' he taunted.

'I'm not going to be in your bed, either, Gabriel!'

Bella did not believe she was going to be in his bed, which, as far as Gabriel was concerned, was a totally different matter. 'You have named your own conditions for our marriage, Isabella,' he rasped. 'Now I wish to tell you mine.'

Her eyes widened. 'You have conditions, too?'

'But of course.' His mouth quirked. 'You did not think that I would allow you to have everything your own way?'

'Forcing me into marrying you is hardly that!' she scorned.

Gabriel gave another shrug. 'You have a choice, Isabella.'

'Not a viable one!'

'No,' he acknowledged simply. 'But it is, nevertheless, still a choice.'

Bella sighed her frustration, just wanting this conversation over and done with now. She was tired, both emotionally and physically, and she needed time and space alone now in which to sit and lick her wounds. While she came to terms with the idea of marrying Gabriel Danti!

How different it would have been if this had happened five years ago. How different Bella would have felt if their night together had been the start of something that had eventually resulted in Gabriel asking her to marry him. She had been so infatuated with him then, so totally seduced by Gabriel's lovemaking, that Bella had absolutely no doubts she would have said yes.

Instead, what they were now proposing was nothing more than a business transaction. A marriage of convenience because both of them wished to ensure that Toby's life, at least, continued in happiness and harmony.

'What's your condition, Gabriel?' she asked.

He didn't answer her immediately, but instead walked slowly towards her, only coming to a halt when he stood mere inches away from her.

Bella eyed him warily, her nails digging into the palms of her hands as she knew herself to be totally aware of the warmth of Gabriel's body, the clean male smell of him, the golden lights that now danced in the warm darkness of his eyes as he looked down at her.

'What do you want?' she snapped apprehensively, to which he gave a slow, seductive smile. A smile Bella took exception to. 'I was referring to your condition, Gabriel,' she added hastily.

'My condition at this moment is one of—'

'Your verbal condition to our marriage!' Bella could see for herself, by the languorous desire burning in that dark gaze as it roamed slowly over the firm thrust of her breasts, and the hard stirring of his body, exactly what Gabriel's physical condition was!

'Ah. Yes. My verbal condition, Isabella,' he murmured, 'is that, in order to ensure the continued harmony of both your own family and mine, I suggest it would be better if they were all to believe that our marriage is a love match.'

Bella gasped in disbelief. 'You want me to *pretend* to be *in love* with you?'

'Only in public,' he qualified.

She glared at him. 'And in private?'

'Oh, simply in lust will do for the moment,' he said softly.

Bella's gaze narrowed. 'You arrogant son-of-a—'

'Insulting my mother will achieve nothing except to annoy me intensely, Isabella,' he warned her.

'I'm so sorry,' she came back sarcastically. 'My intention was to insult *you*, not your mother!'

Gabriel was aroused, not insulted. Marriage to Isabella promised to be a feast for the senses—all of them!

She had been beautiful five years ago, like a delicate and lovely flower that blossomed to his slightest touch. But, Gabriel now realised, he had plundered only one of her petals then. Motherhood and a successful career had ensured there was now so much more to Isabella Scott, and he found it all desirable…

He smiled slowly. 'I am not insulted, Isabella,' he assured huskily. 'Intrigued, perhaps, but not insulted.'

'Pity,' she muttered.

Gabriel's smile widened. 'You agree to my condition, then?'

She eyed him, totally frustrated with her lack of anything resembling control of this situation. 'I assure you I no more want my parents and siblings upset about the choice I'm making than you want to distress your father.'

'And so…?'

She glared her dislike of him, then grudgingly conceded. 'And so, in public at least, I will try to ensure that it appears as if our marriage is something I want.'

'Good.' Gabriel murmured his satisfaction as he lifted his hand and curved it about the delicate line of Bella's jaw, instantly feeling the way she tensed at his lightest touch before moving sharply away. 'Neither your family or my own will be convinced of our—ease with each other, if you react in that way when I touch you!' he growled disapprovingly as his hand fell back to his side.

She gave a dismissive snort. 'I promise I'll try to do better when we have an audience!'

'To merely try is not good enough,' Gabriel told her coldly.

'It's the only answer I can give you for now,' she told him wearily.

Gabriel studied her through narrowed lids, easily able to see that weariness, along with the air of defeat Bella no longer tried to hide from him.

Yes, he had won the battle by forcing Isabella's compliance in the matter of marrying him, and in claiming Toby as his son.

But Gabriel felt little triumph in that victory as he sensed that, in doing so, he might have put the success of the entire war he was waging in jeopardy…

CHAPTER SEVEN

'You make a stunning bride, Bella!' Claudia smiled at her tearfully as she put the finishing touches to the veil before stepping back to admire her sister's appearance.

Bella could only stare numbly at her own reflection, in a beautiful white satin wedding gown and lovely lace veil, in the full-length mirror on the door of the wardrobe in the bedroom that had been hers as a child.

Whoever would have thought, having agreed to Gabriel's marriage proposal, that only five weeks later Bella would be standing here dressed in this beautiful white wedding gown and veil, preparing to drive to the church with her father, on her way to becoming Gabriel's bride?

Gabriel's bride.

Gabriel Danti's bride.

Oh, God!

'You can't be having second thoughts about marrying a man as gorgeous as Gabriel, Bella?' Claudia teased her obvious nervousness.

'No, I can't, can I?' she agreed with forced lightness. 'Go and tell Daddy that I'm ready to leave, hmm?' she asked, waiting until Claudia had left the bedroom before turning back to look at her reflection in the mirror.

What would be the point in having doubts about marrying Gabriel when he had already legally claimed Toby as his son? The name Danti had been enough to ensure that Gabriel's claim was dealt with quickly and positively. Toby Scott was now Tobias Danti.

As Bella would very shortly become Isabella Danti.

Even that name sounded alien to her, not like her at all. Which was pretty apt when Bella hadn't felt like herself for the last five weeks. Even less so today!

The woman reflected in the mirror wearing the white satin gown and delicate lace veil over the dark cascade of her hair certainly looked like her, but Bella could feel no joy in her appearance, or at the thought of becoming Gabriel's wife.

They had shared the news of their engagement with their delighted families five weeks ago. Bella and Toby had then remained in San Francisco for two more days to give Gabriel the time to settle his affairs before he flew back to England with them.

Since arriving in England, Gabriel had been staying in the house in Surrey where Bella had first met him, but coming to the cottage every day in order to spend time with Toby.

When in the company of her family and Gabriel's they had, as agreed, given every impression that they were happy in each other's company.

Not an easy thing on Bella's part when the more time she spent in Gabriel's company, the more physically aware of him she became. Until now, on their wedding day, she felt so tense with that physical awareness it was a constant painful ache. So much for her condition that this was to be a marriage in name only…

This was her wedding day, Bella accepted heavily.

And she couldn't have felt more miserable!

'Where are we going?'

'On our honeymoon, of course,' Gabriel said with satisfaction as he drove the black sports car to the private airfield where the Danti jet was fuelled and waiting to take off, the two of them having just been given a warm send-off by their wedding guests.

'What honeymoon?' Bella frowned as she turned in her seat to look at him, still wearing her wedding gown and veil. 'At no time in the last five weeks did we discuss going away on a honeymoon!'

'We did not discuss it because I knew this would be your reaction if we had,' Gabriel told her unrepentantly.

She scowled her frustration with his high-handed-ness. 'If you knew that then, why—?'

'It was meant to be a surprise,' Gabriel growled.

Her mouth compressed. 'Oh it's certainly that all right.'

'It is Toby's surprise, Bella,' he elaborated softly.

She looked at him sharply. 'Toby's?'

Gabriel nodded. 'Our son confided in me several weeks ago that newly married people go away on honeymoon together after the wedding.'

Bella's cheeks were flushed. 'You should have ex-plained to him—'

'Should have explained *what* exactly to him, Isabella?' Gabriel grated harshly. 'That although his mother and father are now married, they are not in love with each other? That his mother has no desire what-soever to spend time alone with his father?'

Bella winced. When he put it like that…!

They had spent the last few weeks, individually and together, convincing Toby that they were all going to be happy as a real family. Obviously they had succeeded as far as Toby was concerned, which was why he had decided his parents going away on honeymoon together was what a 'real family' did…

'I don't have any other clothes with me—'

'Claudia was kind enough to pack a suitcase for you,' Gabriel explained. 'It is in the trunk of the car with my own.'

Well, that explained the mischievous glint Bella had seen in Claudia's eyes earlier as her sister had stood with the other wedding guests outside the hotel to wave them off!

'Toby also arranged to stay with your parents for the week we are away,' Gabriel supplied. 'With my father remaining in England and visiting him often.'

'He's certainly been busy, hasn't he?' Bella sighed as she raised her hands to take the pins out of her hair and remove the veil, her head throbbing. 'That's better.' She threw the veil onto the back seat before sitting back more comfortably.

This really had been the most difficult day of Bella's life. Starting with the conversation her father had insisted on having with her early this morning…

He had been alone in the kitchen drinking coffee when Bella had come downstairs at six-thirty, his con-versation light as she had made herself a cup of coffee.

Once Bella had sat down at the kitchen table with him it had been a different matter, however.

He had gently voiced his own and her mother's worries about the haste with which Bella and Gabriel were getting married. Was she doing the right thing? Was she really sure this was what she wanted? There was no doubting Toby's excitement but was Bella going to be happy?

Lying to her father had possibly been the hardest thing Bella had ever done.

Even now, thinking of his gentle concern for her happiness, Bella could feel the tears prick her eyes. 'So, where have you decided we're going on our honeymoon?' she asked Gabriel heavily.

Gabriel's mouth tightened at the fatigue in Bella's tone as she made no effort to hide the fact that today had been no more than a trial she'd had to get through.

She had looked stunningly beautiful as she had walked down the aisle towards him. A vision in white satin and lace.

A vision in white satin and lace who had avoided so much as meeting his gaze. Whose voice had quivered with uncertainty as she made her vows, her hand trembling slightly as she allowed Gabriel to slide the thin gold wedding band in place. Her fingers had been cold as she'd placed the matching gold band Gabriel had insisted on upon his own finger, her mouth stiff and unresponsive as Gabriel kissed her to seal their vows. Although admittedly she had made an effort to smile and acknowledge their guests as they'd walked back down the aisle together as husband and wife.

Probably because looking and smiling at their guests

was preferable to looking at him, Gabriel acknowledged grimly to himself.

'We are flying to your island in the Caribbean,' Gabriel told her.

'Don't you mean *your* island in the Caribbean?' she corrected.

'No, I mean yours,' Gabriel said. 'It is my wedding gift to you.' He hadn't meant to tell her that quite so abruptly; had intended surprising her with his gift once they arrived at their destination. He would have stuck to that plan, too, if he weren't feeling quite so frustrated with her distant behaviour.

Bella was absolutely stunned as she stared at Gabriel in complete disbelief. Gabriel was giving her a whole island in the Caribbean as a wedding present?

His mouth quirked as he obviously read some of her incredulity. 'Do not look so concerned, Isabella. It is only a small island.'

'Isn't even a *small* island a little overkill when I only gave you a pair of cufflinks?' A frown marred her brow.

Bella had only bought the cufflinks at the last moment because Claudia, as Chief Bridesmaid, said she had to; until then Bella hadn't even thought of giving Gabriel a gift to mark their marriage. What could she possibly give to the man who had everything?

Although Bella had noted, as they stood together in the church, that Gabriel was wearing the diamond and onyx links in the cuffs of the pristine white shirt he wore beneath the dark grey frock coat…

'You have given me so much more than that, Isabella,' Gabriel assured her huskily.

She looked at him warily, but she was unable to read

anything from his expression. 'I don't know what you mean,' she finally murmured uncertainly.

'I am talking of Toby, Isabella. You have given me a son,' he explained evenly.

A man who had everything—except that...

'Wow, a wedding ring and an island in the Caribbean,' she mocked. 'What would you have given me if I had only produced a daughter? A monthly allowance and visiting rights, perhaps?'

'No, I would have given you a wedding ring and an island in the Caribbean!' A nerve pulsed in Gabriel's cheek as he answered her. 'I would value a daughter no less than a son, Isabella, and I have no idea why you would ever think that I might. Or why it is you take such delight in insulting me!'

Why *did* Bella take delight in insulting him?

Because she was angry with him. Because she was angry with herself. Because she was just plain angry!

She was angry with Gabriel for forcing her into this marriage.

She was angry with herself for allowing him to do so.

She was angry because a part of her had thrilled at the sight of Gabriel as he'd stood down the aisle waiting for her, looking so devastatingly handsome in the dark frock coat and white shirt and red bow tie. She was angry because her voice had quivered with emotion as she had made her vows to him and because her hand had trembled at his slightest touch as he'd placed his wedding ring upon her finger.

Bella was angry for all of those reasons and more!

'I'm sorry,' she sighed wearily. 'It's been a long and—and difficult day.'

'For both of us,' Gabriel pointed out.

'Yes.' Bella turned her head to look at him.

Gabriel looked as strained as she felt, Bella acknowledged ruefully, lines beside his eyes and the grimness of his mouth, his skin slightly pale beneath his naturally olive complexion.

How different this could all have been if Gabriel hadn't been in love with another woman five years ago. How different today could have been if the two of them had married because they were in love with each other now.

Instead they were two strangers who had married to protect and sustain their young son's happiness.

Bella swallowed hard. 'I think, if you don't mind, that I would like to just sit here quietly for a while.' She closed her eyes.

Gabriel did mind. If Bella thought the last five weeks had been any less of a strain for him, then she was mistaken.

In company, Bella had managed, as agreed, to maintain an air of tranquil happiness, but once they were alone it had been a totally different matter. She had shown a total lack of interest whenever he had tried to discuss the wedding arrangements with her. Had been uncommunicative on the three Sunday mornings they had attended church together in order to hear the reading of their Banns.

Worst of all, once they were alone, Bella had avoided so much as touching him…

If Bella wished to punish him for forcing this marriage on her then she could not have chosen a better way to do it than with her icy silence and her obvious aversion to his lightest touch!

* * *

'You and your father certainly know how to travel in style,' Bella commented lightly as she sat across the table from Gabriel in the luxurious cabin of the Danti jet, only now beginning to appreciate the wealth and power behind the Danti name.

Well…apart from earlier when Gabriel had informed her he had given her an island in the Caribbean as a wedding gift!

Bella shied away from even thinking about what she was going to do with an island in the Caribbean and instead turned her attention back to her present surroundings.

The Danti-owned jet was the height of luxury, only six ultra-comfortable seats in the spacious and carpeted main cabin, with a bar at the cockpit end, and a door to another private compartment at the other.

Gabriel had given instructions to the captain to take off as soon as they were on board and their luggage had been stowed in the cabin at the back of the plane. A male steward had then placed two long-stemmed fluted glasses on the glass table in front of them before pouring the bubbly champagne, leaving the bottle cooling in a bucket of ice beside Gabriel and then disappearing back into the galley behind the bar and closing the door discreetly behind him.

Bella had totally avoided even looking at her own glass of champagne as it reminded her all too forcibly of that night with Gabriel five years ago. The last thing she needed to think about at the moment was that!

Gabriel nodded now. 'As you and Toby will also do now that you are Dantis.'

The sinking feeling in Bella's stomach owed nothing

to air-sickness and everything to the realisation that that was who she really was now.

Isabella Danti. Wife of Gabriel.

'No doubt Toby will be impressed,' she answered.

'But not you?'

Bella was more nervous than impressed. Nervous of being really alone with Gabriel for the first time in five weeks. A quivering wreck just at the thought of spending a week alone with him on *her* Caribbean island.

She shook her head. 'I'm not four years old, Gabriel.'

'No, you are not, are you?'

Bella shot Gabriel a swift glance, not in the least re-assured by the intensity of his chocolate-brown eyes as his gaze met hers and held it captive.

She physically had to turn her head away to break that gaze before she could stand up abruptly. 'I—I think I would like to go into the other room and take off this wedding gown.'

'An excellent idea, Isabella,' Gabriel murmured huskily.

Bella frowned up at him as he rose slowly to his feet, his height and the width of his shoulders at once dominating the cabin. 'I think I'm quite capable of changing my clothes on my own, thank you,' she told him sharply.

Gabriel gave a mocking inclination of his head. 'I thought you might need some help with the zip at the back of your gown.'

Good point, Bella realised. The wedding gown was medieval in style, with long, close-fitting lace sleeves that tapered to a point at her wrist, their snug fit making it impossible for Bella to reach the zip that ran the whole length of her spine without risking ripping the sleeves at the seams. It hadn't been a problem earlier today, because Claudia had helped her to dress, but Bella couldn't say she was exactly comfortable now with the thought of Gabriel helping her to *un*dress…

Comfortable? The thought of Gabriel touching her at all was enough to send her already fractured nerves into a complete tailspin!

She was never going to wear this gown again anyway, so what did it matter if she *did* rip the sleeves?

'I'm sure I can manage, thank you,' she replied distantly as she turned away.

'I need to change into less formal clothing, too,' Gabriel insisted quietly as he reached the door to the back compartment before Bella and held it open for her to enter.

Bella looked up at him uncertainly, knowing by the hard challenge she could see in his eyes that Gabriel expected to continue—and that he was actually enjoying!—arguing with her. On the basis that some sort of response from her was better than none, perhaps? Probably, Bella acknowledged wryly, even as she experienced a perverse desire not to give him that satisfaction.

'Fine,' she accepted airily before striding past him into the cabin at the back of the plane.

Only to come to an abrupt halt as she found herself, not in another sitting-room as she had supposed, but in a room totally dominated by the king-size bed in its centre!

Gabriel's eyes darkened with amusement when he saw Bella's stunned expression as she took in the luxuriously appointed bedroom with its fitted wardrobes, gold thick-piled carpet, and the deep gold and cream silk linen that covered the bed, several throw cushions of the same rich material against the sumptuous pillows.

Unfortunately Bella didn't stay stunned for very long as she turned to look up at him accusingly. 'I hope you don't have any ideas about adding my name to the list of women you've no doubt seduced in here!' she snapped.

Gabriel's humour faded at the deliberate insult. 'You have the tongue of a viper!'

She raised mocking brows. 'It's a little late for second thoughts, don't you think, Gabriel? We were married earlier today, remember?'

'Oh, I remember, Isabella,' he rasped harshly. 'Perhaps it is time that I reminded you of that fact also!' He closed the door gently behind him.

Bella took a step back as she obviously read the intent in his eyes. 'I meant what I said, Gabriel—I am not about to become another notch on your mile-high bedpost!'

Gabriel's jaw clenched as he took that same step forward. 'I meant what I said five weeks ago, too, concerning the right to change your mind about our marriage being in name only!'

Her eyes widened in alarm. 'Not here!'

'Wherever and whenever,' he promised.

She backed away from him. 'I told you I will not become another notch—'

'If you look at the bed again, Isabella, you will see that there is no bedpost.' Gabriel's voice was dangerously soft. 'And we are at least three miles high.'

'Your three-mile-high club, then,' she persisted as she faced him bravely, only the uncertainty Gabriel could read in her eyes telling him of the nervousness Bella was trying so desperately to hide.

Gabriel took another step forward, standing only inches away from Bella now, and able to see the nerve pulsing at the base of her throat and the slight trembling of her lips.

Full pouting lips that were slightly parted, that perfect bow of a top lip a temptation, the bottom one becoming a lure as the tip of Bella's tongue moved moistly between them.

An invitation, whether Bella meant it to be so, that Gabriel had no intention of resisting!

'Turn around, Isabella, so that I can unzip your gown,' he suggested gruffly.

She swallowed hard. 'I don't—' She broke off with a gasp as Gabriel ignored her protest and stepped behind her. She felt the touch of his fingers as he slowly began to slide the zip down.

Bella's second protest went unspoken, her back arching involuntarily as she felt the delicious ripples of awareness through her whole body as that zip slowly— so very slowly—moved down the length of her spine, her breath catching in her throat as Gabriel parted the satin material and she felt the warm caress of his lips against the bareness of her shoulder.

Desire. She instantly felt a hot, burning desire that ripped through her body at the first touch of Gabriel's mouth against her heated flesh, the moist rasp of his tongue as he licked and tasted her only intensifying that burning heat.

Much as she denied it, much as she fought against it, Bella knew she wanted him.

Wanted Gabriel passionately.

Knew that she had been fighting that want, that need, for the last five weeks, afraid to even touch him in case she revealed that ever-escalating desire. With the result that each minute she spent in his company had been torture, and full of an aching desire that had always seemed only seconds away from release.

It was a passion that Bella had only been able to keep in check by presenting Gabriel with a veneer of icy coldness. An icy veneer that had melted with the force of an avalanche the moment his mouth touched her naked flesh!

Her neck arched, her head resting back against Gabriel's shoulder as his hands slid inside the unzipped gown to move about her waist and then higher as he cupped the nakedness of her breasts beneath the satin gown, her own hands moving up to rest on top of his as she pressed him into her, wanting his caresses.

She cried out, desire surging between her thighs as Gabriel's thumbs moved across her turgid nipples, her body taut with expectation, not able to breathe as she waited for the second caress, gasping, almost sobbing as Gabriel's lips moved heatedly, moistly against her throat as he took those throbbing peaks between his thumbs and fingers and squeezed rhythmically.

'Gabriel?' Bella groaned as her bottom moved against the hardness of his arousal. 'Gabriel, please...!'

'Not yet, Bella,' Gabriel refused huskily even though his own body throbbed with that same need for release.

They had a long flight ahead of them, hours and hours before they reached their destination, and before that happened Gabriel intended to discover and fulfil every one of Bella's fantasies, as he hoped that she would fulfil every one of his.

Stripping the white satin wedding gown from Bella's body was only the first of the fantasies that had kept him awake night after night for the last five weeks!

Gabriel heard her moan of protest as he slowly moved his hands from inside her gown, her breath catching in her throat seconds later as she realised he had only done so in order to slide the gown from her shoulders and down her arms before he bared her to the waist and then slowly allowed the gown to pool on the floor at her feet.

Bella's eyes were closed and Gabriel stared down at how beautiful she looked in only a pair of brief white lace panties and white stockings.

Her throat was exposed, her lips slightly parted and moist, her lids half closing over eyes of deep purple as Gabriel's arms moved about her and his hands once again cupped her breasts before his thumbs moved to caress the deep rose nipples.

'Yes!' she exclaimed. 'Oh, God, yes, Gabriel…!'

Gabriel pulled her back against him so his lips could roam freely, erotically up the length of her throat to the sensitivity of her ear lobe, his teeth nibbling on that lobe even as one hand continued to caress the firmness of a perfect nipple and his other hand moved lower still.

Bella's skin felt like velvet as his fingers splayed across the bare expanse of her waist and down over the jut of her hip. Gabriel opened his eyes to look down to where his hand cupped and teased her breast, his own skin so much darker than the creamy magnolia of hers.

His teeth bit the softness of her ear lobe even as his gaze moved lower to where his fingers quested beneath the silk of her panties to the dark curls he could see clearly through the sheerness of the material, parting the dampness of those curls and seeking the sensitive nub nestled amongst their darkness. Seeking and finding as his fingers began to stroke her there.

She was so hot and slick, her sensitive folds swollen with need, a need Gabriel intended building until Bella cried out, begged for him to give her the climax her body craved.

Bella moaned low in her throat as she felt the brush of Gabriel's fingers against her, her legs parting to allow him greater access, an invitation he accepted as he plunged one long, satisfying finger deep inside her, followed by another as his thumb continued to stroke against her swollen nub and his other hand squeezed and caressed her breast in the same mind-blowing rhythm.

Again and again.

Those caresses becoming fiercer. Deeper. Faster.

The heat rose unbearably, building, growing ever stronger as Bella's hips moved to meet the deep thrust of Gabriel's fingers inside her.

'Don't stop, Gabriel!' she gasped breathlessly. 'Please don't stop!'

'Let go, Bella!' he groaned hoarsely against her throat. 'Give yourself, *cara*!'

'Yes…' she breathed raggedly. 'Oh, yes! Oh, God, yes…!' Bella gasped and writhed against Gabriel's hand as her climax surged out of control and wave after wave of burning, shattering pleasure rippled through her.

Gabriel held her captive as his fingers continued to

pleasure her, Bella climaxing again and again, her body quivering and shaking at Gabriel's slightest touch.

'No more, Gabriel!' she finally sobbed as she collapsed weakly in his arms.

CHAPTER EIGHT

BELLA woke slowly, slightly disorientated as she looked around the unfamiliar room.

And then she remembered.

Not just where she was, but everything that had happened since she had entered this bedroom.

Bella turned her face into the pillows, the aching protest of her body as she curled into a foetal position reminding her all too forcefully of the way Gabriel had touched and caressed her.

So much for her claim, her determination, that her marriage to Gabriel would be in name only—they hadn't even left British airspace before she'd succumbed to his caresses!

It was—

She looked sharply towards the door as she heard the handle turning softly before it was opened, her expression becoming defensive as she saw Gabriel standing in the doorway.

The cream polo shirt and jeans he wore showed that he had remained in the bedroom long enough to change his clothes after Bella—after she—After she what? Collapsed from the sheer ecstasy Gabriel had given her time and time again until she simply couldn't take any more?

Oh, God…!

Her mouth tightened. 'If you've come to gloat—'

'I came to see if you were awake yet,' he corrected coldly. 'We will be landing shortly, and you need time to dress before we do.'

Which reminded Bella all too forcibly that she was completely naked—apart from her panties and hold-up stockings—beneath the bedclothes.

It also reminded her that although she had been almost naked Gabriel had remained completely dressed throughout their earlier— Their earlier what? Sexual encounter? Lovemaking? It could hardly be called the latter when there was no love for each other, on either side.

Sexual encounter, then.

How awful did that sound?

'Thank you,' she accepted with polite dismissal.

Gabriel scowled across the cabin at Bella for several long seconds. Knowing her as he did, he hadn't been expecting her to fall lovingly into his arms when she awoke, but her coldness, her accusation that he had come here to gloat over her earlier capitulation, was unforgivable.

His expression was grim as he crossed the cabin in three long strides to stand beside the bed and look down at her. 'It is not me you are angry with, Isabella—'

'Don't presume to tell me what I'm feeling,' she said resentfully, her eyes glittering with suppressed emotion as she glowered up at him.

Gabriel sat down on the side of the bed, trapping her beneath the bedclothes as he put a hand either side of her to lean over her. 'We are husband and wife, Isabella; there is absolutely no reason for you to feel embarrassed because of what happened between us earlier—'

'I'm not *embarrassed*, Gabriel—I'm *disgusted*. With myself as much as with you!' she added, her expression defiant as she met his gaze squarely.

Gabriel wanted to reach out and shake her out of this mood of self-recrimination. But if he were to touch her again now, even in anger, he knew that he wouldn't be able to stop himself from making love with her again.

Just looking at Bella, her hair a cloud of darkness against the gold colour of the pillows, her mouth a sensual pout, and knowing her body was almost completely naked beneath the bedclothes was enough to make Gabriel shift uncomfortably as his thighs became engorged with arousal. His own lack of release earlier had become an aching throb he'd remained totally aware of while Bella slept.

He stood up abruptly, needing to put some distance between himself and Bella before speaking again, but before he could do so she got in first. 'Just don't count on a repeat performance, Gabriel,' she snapped.

Where Bella was concerned Gabriel didn't take anything for granted. Not one single thing. 'We will be landing in ten minutes, Isabella, so I suggest that before we do you get some clothes on,' he bit out tersely.

She kept the covers pulled up against her as she sat up, her hair falling silkily about her shoulders. 'I thought you said it was a small Caribbean island?'

'It is,' Gabriel confirmed. 'We will complete the rest of our journey by helicopter.'

Bella had never been in a helicopter before, and wasn't sure how she was going to respond to being in such a small aircraft.

She was even less comfortable when she realised that Gabriel intended piloting the small black wasp-looking craft himself!

She looked at him uncertainly as he climbed into the seat beside her after stowing their cases in the back. 'Are you sure you know how to fly one of these things?'

'Very sure,' he drawled. 'I assure you, Isabella, you will be completely safe in my hands,' he added mockingly as she still didn't look convinced.

Bella shot him a narrow-eyed glare before turning away to look out of the window beside her at the bright sunshine reflecting on the beautiful blue-green ocean beyond a beach of white-gold sand.

A relaxed pose that didn't last any longer than it took for Gabriel to start the engine and move the controls to lift the helicopter from the ground!

Bella reached out to clutch at Gabriel's arm as the helicopter bucked and swayed as it rose into the air. 'I think I'm going to be sick!' she cried frantically.

'You will not be sick if you look out at the sea and not down at the ground,' he instructed.

Easy enough for him to say, Bella groaned inwardly as her stomach continued to heave in protest for several long minutes, only settling down to a slight queasiness as the helicopter levelled out and she could finally appreciate the beauty of the scenery.

The sun was bright and very hot, the sea so blue and clear that Bella could see the sandy bottom in several places, even more so as they began to approach a small island edged by unspoilt beautiful beaches and covered in lush green foliage and trees.

Gabriel flew the helicopter over the beach, almost but not quite touching the tops of the trees, Bella's eyes widening as she saw he was heading towards a white-painted villa on top of a hill, only slightly inland and surrounded by more trees and huge brightly coloured flowers.

'Home.' Gabriel nodded in answer to Bella's questioning look as he began to lower the helicopter onto the patch of flat green grass next to the villa. 'What did you expect, Bella?' He turned to her once they were down on the ground. 'That I was bringing you to a shack in the middle of nowhere?'

Bella hadn't really given a lot of thought as to where they would stay once they reached the island. The fact that Gabriel had given her an island as a wedding gift had seemed fantastic enough!

'It is slightly primitive in that there are no servants here to wait on us,' Gabriel warned.

Bella smiled wryly. 'I won't miss what I've never had, Gabriel.'

'A Frenchman owned the island previously, and he had the villa built several years ago,' Gabriel told her as he climbed out of the helicopter. 'Obviously, if you want to change the décor then you must do so.'

'It's beautiful as it is,' Bella murmured as she took her sunglasses off to follow him inside the villa.

The floors were cool cream-and-terracotta-coloured marble, the cream furniture in the sitting-room kept to a minimum, with several glass-topped tables placed conveniently beside the armchairs and sofa. The kitchen was even more surprising, everything white, including the cooker and huge refrigerator and freezer.

'We have our own generator and fresh water supply,' Gabriel told her as she moved slowly about the room. 'Or rather, you have your own generator and fresh water supply,' he corrected ruefully.

Bella blinked, totally overwhelmed now that she was actually here. 'This really is all *mine*?'

Gabriel nodded. 'Do you like it?' His expression was guarded.

Almost as if he expected her to throw his gift back in his face. Not literally, of course, but verbally at least. Not surprising considering her remarks when Gabriel had first told her about the island!

'I love it!' Bella assured him emotionally. 'I—thank you, Gabriel,' she added slightly breathlessly.

Gabriel stood across the kitchen, his own sunglasses pushed up into the darkness of his hair. Hair that he hadn't bothered to have cut the last five weeks, its longer length making him look more like the man Bella had met and briefly fallen for five years ago.

She turned away abruptly. 'How on earth did everything get here? The materials to build the villa? The furniture?' she quickly asked to cover her sudden and complete awareness of Gabriel as he stood there so still and yet so lethally attractive.

Gabriel shrugged. 'The same way that the food in the freezer and refrigerator got here.' He opened the fridge door to show her all the food stored on the shelves. 'By boat,' he supplied ruefully as Bella still looked puzzled.

Bella eyes narrowed. 'Are you telling me that I didn't

have to suffer that helicopter flight at all? That we could have come here by *boat*, instead?'

Gabriel held back a smile at her slightly indignant expression. 'I thought it would be more…dramatic… to arrive by helicopter,' he admitted.

'Oh, you did, did you…?' Bella said quietly as she placed her bag down on one of the work-surfaces.

'I did, yes,' Gabriel muttered warily, not able to read Bella's mood at all as she strolled over and opened the freezer door, taking out a tray of ice cubes before moving over to the sink. 'Of course, you must be thirsty,' he acknowledged. 'There is a selection of drinks in the— What are you doing?' He frowned as Bella approached him brandishing a handful of ice cubes before reaching out to grasp the collar of his polo shirt and dropping them inside. 'Bella!' Gabriel gasped in protest at the first uncomfortable touch of the icy-cold cubes against the heat of his flesh.

'I thought you were looking a little hot, Gabriel,' she drawled as he stepped back to shake the frozen cubes out of his clothing, several of them shattering on the marble floor.

'Damn it, Bella—' Gabriel broke off as Bella began to laugh at his discomfort.

It was the first time, Gabriel realised, that he had heard her laugh without cynicism or sarcasm since they'd met again five weeks ago.

His breath caught in his throat as he stared at her, those gorgeous violet eyes shining with good humour, her teeth tiny and white against her pale pink lip gloss, a healthy colour in her cheeks.

Bella was the most beautiful woman Gabriel had ever seen!

'Perhaps I deserved that,' he allowed gruffly.

'Perhaps you did,' she confirmed unrepentantly. 'Next time we come by boat, yes?' she said as she moved to pick up the shattered ice cubes.

Gabriel remained silent as he hunkered down on his haunches to help her, unwilling to break the sudden truce by making any comment that Bella might take exception to, satisfied for the moment that there would be a next time…

'What are you doing, Gabriel?'

He threw his cheroot to the ground, grinding it beneath the sole of his shoe before turning slowly to look at Bella as she stood behind him in the moonlight.

Their uneasy truce had continued while they walked along the beach earlier, and through the dinner they had prepared together and then eaten outside on the terrace that overlooked the moon-dappled ocean. The two of them had returned outside after they had cleared the dishes away, the silence between them companionable rather than awkward as they finished drinking the bottle of red wine Gabriel had opened to accompany their meal.

Bella had excused herself half an hour or so ago in order to go to the master bedroom to prepare for bed, Gabriel opting to stay outside a little longer, still reluctant to say or do anything that might shatter even the illusion of the companionship they had found together since the ice-cube incident.

They were due to stay here for a week, and Gabriel

would prefer that they not spend all of that time at loggerheads!

Looking at Bella now, in a pale-lilac-coloured night-gown, the silk material clinging to her breasts and moulding to the gentle curve of her hips, Gabriel knew that he wanted to strip even that flimsy garment from her before making love with her.

Something, after her comments earlier on the plane, that was sure to shatter even the illusion of companionship that they'd shared so far!

He thrust his hands into the pockets of the black trousers he had changed into before dinner. 'I thought you would prefer your privacy after such a long and tiring day.'

Bella looked at him searchingly, but was totally unable to read Gabriel's mood beneath the remoteness of his expression. 'Aren't you coming to bed?' she finally prompted hesitantly.

'Later, perhaps,' he rasped dismissively. 'I am not tired yet.'

Bella hadn't exactly had sleep in mind when she'd asked that question!

The island was beautiful, and totally unspoilt, she had discovered as she and Gabriel had strolled barefooted, if slightly apart, along the shoreline before dinner. The water had lapped gently against their feet, the smell of the exotic blossoms wafting in the warm softness of the breeze, and all adding to the seduction of the evening.

To the air of awareness that lay hidden just below the surface of even the slightest glance that Bella and Gabriel exchanged.

At least, she had thought it had.

Gabriel's reluctance to come to bed now seemed to imply that only she had felt that aching awareness.

Because Gabriel's lovemaking earlier had only been a way of showing her that he really could make love to her wherever and whenever *he* felt like it, as he had put it so bluntly?

That, having already proved his point once today, Gabriel now felt no urgency to repeat the experience?

How utterly ridiculous of her to have imagined that, because the two of them hadn't argued for the last few hours, they could have actually reached some sort of understanding in their relationship. Gabriel had never made any secret of his reason for marrying her—his only reason for marrying her!—and that reason was Toby.

Bella felt the humiliated colour burn her cheeks. 'You're right, Gabriel, I would prefer my privacy,' she said. 'As such, it would be better if you used one of the other bedrooms, and kept out of mine, for the duration of our stay here.'

Gabriel's gaze narrowed on the pale oval of her face in the moonlight, her chin raised in challenge, that same challenge reflected in the deep purple of her eyes.

'Don't come any closer, Gabriel!' she warned as he took a step towards her.

A warning Gabriel chose to ignore as he came to stand only inches away from her, his eyes glittering darkly as he looked down the length of his arrogant nose at her, and his hands clenched at his sides as he obviously fought the urge to reach out and shake her until her teeth rattled.

Bella felt her own anger starting to fade as she instead found herself fascinated by the nerve that pulsed beside that livid scar on Gabriel's tautly clenched left cheek.

He looked so gloriously handsome with his long hair slightly tousled onto his shoulders, the black silk shirt and tailored trousers only adding to that darkness, his eyes also appearing a glittering black in the moonlight.

Bella had never known another man with the grace and beauty of Gabriel. Had never been as physically aware of another man in the way she was Gabriel. Had never wanted another man in the way she constantly seemed to want Gabriel.

As, God help her, she wanted him even now…!

She swallowed hard. 'You're right, Gabriel, it's been a long and tiring day. Far too long and tiring for this conversation,' she said huskily. 'I—I'll wish you a goodnight.'

His mouth twisted self-derisively. 'I very much doubt that it will be that!'

Bella looked at him searchingly for several seconds before shaking her head ruefully. 'We really must try to find a way to stop insulting each other, Gabriel.'

He winced. 'The only time we manage to do that is when we are making love together, but…' He shrugged. 'Goodnight, Isabella. I will try not to wake you when I come to bed.'

Bella was frowning as she turned and walked slowly back inside the villa, too utterly weary to fight him any more concerning their sleeping arrangements. Especially as Gabriel had already made it plain she would lose!

She very much doubted that she would be able to fall

asleep when she knew that at any moment Gabriel would be coming to share what was now *their* bed.

Very much doubted that she would be able to sleep at all with Gabriel in bed beside her...

CHAPTER NINE

'DO YOU know how to scuba-dive, Isabella?'

'No.' Bella looked up from eating her piece of toast as she and Gabriel sat outside on the veranda eating their breakfast. 'Do you?'

As Bella had already guessed, it had not been a restful night's sleep, and she had still been awake but pretending not to be when Gabriel had joined her in the bedroom half an hour or so after she had gone to bed. That Gabriel had fallen asleep within minutes of his head resting on the pillow had made absolutely no difference to her own feelings of tension, and Bella had lain awake for hours after the even tenor of Gabriel's breathing told her he remained fast asleep beside her.

Bella's only consolation was that Gabriel was already up and making breakfast when she finally woke up shortly after nine o'clock. But her eyes still felt gritty from lack of sleep, and all she really felt like doing was going back to bed!

'I would hardly have asked otherwise,' Gabriel pointed out before taking a sip of his coffee. 'Would you like to learn?'

He looked disgustingly well rested this morning in a white short-sleeved shirt and white trousers, Bella noted, disgruntled. Much more relaxed than he had a right to be, as far as she was concerned.

'I suppose I could try,' she agreed irritably. 'As long as you aren't one of those awful teachers who gets cross with their student.'

'I have no doubts you will be a very attentive pupil, Isabella,' Gabriel teased, knowing by the heavy look to her eyes and the weary droop of her mouth that she hadn't slept well.

Gabriel had known she was still awake when he joined her in the bed the night before, her back firmly turned towards him as she had tried to give every appearance of being asleep. A deception Gabriel had allowed her to keep; it was enough for the moment that she accepted that they would be sharing a bed in future.

She gave him a sharp glance. 'I sincerely hope you were referring to scuba-diving!'

'What else?' he taunted.

Bella continued to eye him suspiciously for several long seconds, and then she gave a dismissive shrug. 'Why not? I obviously have nothing else to do today.' She stood up suddenly.

Gabriel looked up at her searchingly. 'Perhaps you would have preferred to go somewhere a little more…entertaining…for our honeymoon?'

Bella raked him with a scathing glance. 'Oh, I think this is entertaining enough, don't you?'

He laughed softly. 'Let us hope so.'

Bella refused to meet the challenge in his gaze. 'I'll go and get changed.'

Although she wasn't too sure about that once she saw the skimpiness of the bikinis that Claudia, obviously in on the secret of their honeymoon destination, had packed for her!

There were two of them. A black one that consisted of two very small scraps of material that barely covered anything, top or bottom. And a pink one, which admittedly had a little more material in the bottom half, but unfortunately the top plunged deeply at the front, meaning that when she put it on her breasts spilled over it revealingly.

Quite what Claudia had been thinking of when she chose them, Bella had no idea—but she could take a good guess.

Bella forgot her own self-consciousness in the pink bikini the instant she came out onto the terrace and saw that Gabriel was wearing the briefest—and sexiest— pair of black swimming trunks she had ever seen!

Fitting low down on his hips, the material barely covered that revealing bulge in the front of the trunks. A bulge Bella found it difficult to look away from…

Gabriel looked up from checking the scuba gear, his expression hardening as he saw the way Bella was staring at him. 'Do my scars bother you, after all?' he ground out harshly.

'Scars?' she repeated vaguely, trying to concentrate on something other than those skimpy bathing trunks. 'Oh. Those scars.' She nodded as she took in the revealing criss-cross of scars that marked his chest and back, several deeper marks that looked like surgical incisions on his left leg, both below and above the knee. 'I've already told you they don't bother me, Gabriel,' she said with a frown.

'That was before you had seen the full extent of them,' he said stiltedly. 'Some women would be bothered by their unsightliness.'

Some women *would*? Or they already *had*? Perhaps Janine Childe, for instance…?

Bella stepped outside. 'We all have scars, Gabriel. It's just that some of us have them on the inside rather than the outside. Besides,' she continued as he would have spoken, 'what does it matter to you how I feel about them?'

Gabriel's eyes were narrowed to dark slits. 'You are the woman who will have to look at them for the rest of your life.'

The rest of her life?

She took a deep breath as she realised she hadn't actually thought about her marriage to Gabriel with exactly that time-frame in mind before…

She suddenly realised she hadn't said anything and Gabriel was still waiting… 'I wouldn't worry about it, Gabriel. All men look the same in the dark—' She broke off as Gabriel's hands suddenly closed firmly about her upper arms. 'Let go of me!' she gasped.

His grasp didn't relax in the slightest. 'I am not interested in what you think of other men, Isabella. In the dark or otherwise!' He shook her slightly, his expression now distinctly dangerous.

Bella stared up at him, unable to see anything but the darkness of his anger as he glared down at her. 'Your scars don't bother me, Gabriel, and that's the truth,' she finally said evenly.

His gaze remained dark and stormy on her face for several more seconds before he released her so suddenly that Bella stumbled slightly. 'I will be several more minutes checking the scuba equipment, so perhaps you would like to go for a swim while you are waiting,' he suggested abruptly.

Bella gave one last, lingering glance at the stiffness of his scarred back before turning away to walk in the direction of the beach.

Another day in paradise…

'That was the most wonderful experience of my life!' Bella gasped excitedly once she had waded out of the sea and removed her breathing mask.

'The *most* wonderful?' Gabriel arched mocking brows as he removed his own scuba gear before sitting down on the blanket spread on the white-gold sand, the long darkness of his hair pushed back from his face, rivulets of sea-water dripping enticingly down his shoulders and back.

'Well…one of them,' Bella corrected hastily. 'Holding Toby in my arms seconds after he was born was probably the most wonderful,' she added huskily.

A frown darkened Gabriel's brow. 'I would have liked to have shared that experience with you.'

'It's been a lovely day, Gabriel, let's not spoil it with another argument.' Bella sighed as she dropped down onto the blanket beside him before slipping her arms out of the straps of the scuba gear and dropping it back on the sand behind them. She pushed the dampness of her hair back over her shoulders and sat forward to clasp her arms about her knees and rest her chin on her bent knees. 'Besides, I very much doubt even you would have been allowed into the delivery-room.'

Gabriel arched one dark brow. 'Even me…?'

She nodded. 'Not even the Danti name would have got you in there,' she teased. 'There was a bit of a scare at the last moment,' she explained as Gabriel continued to look at her enquiringly. 'My blood pressure went off the scale, Toby became distressed, and they had to rush me off to Theatre to deliver Toby by Caesarean section.'

Gabriel tensed. 'Your life was in danger?'

'I think both our lives were in danger for a while,' Bella admitted. 'But luckily it all turned out okay in the end.'

The frown between Gabriel's eyes didn't lessen. 'Is that likely to happen with a second pregnancy?'

Bella gave him a surprised glance. 'I don't know. It never occurred to me to ask. Gabriel?' She stared at him as he stood up abruptly to walk the short distance to the water's edge. 'Gabriel, what's wrong?'

Gabriel's hands clenched at his sides. Bella could ask him that, when she might have lost her life giving birth to Toby? When they might both have lost their lives and he, Gabriel, Bella's lover and Toby's father, would not have even known!

'The way I see it, both you and I have almost died and have the scars to prove it—' Bella broke off abruptly as Gabriel turned, his expression fierce. 'I was only trying to make light of the situation, Gabriel,' she reasoned.

His eyes narrowed to steely slits. 'You think the risk to your life is a subject for humour?'

She grimaced. 'I think it's something that happened four and a half years ago. It's nothing but history now. We're all still here, after all.'

Gabriel knew that Bella was right, but having just learnt that she might have died giving birth to Toby made him wonder—fear?—that a second pregnancy might be as dangerous...

'May I see your scar?'

Bella looked up at Gabriel warily as he loomed over her and blocked out the sun, his face darkly intense.

He wanted to see her scar from the Caesarean section? Her below-the-bikini-line scar?

She swallowed hard. 'Can't you just take my word for it that it's there?'

There was a slight easing of the tension in his expression. 'No.'

'Oh.' Bella chewed on her bottom lip. 'I would really rather not.' Her arms tightened protectively about her knees.

'Why not?'

Because it was far too intimate, that was why! Because she already felt totally exposed, vulnerable, in the brief bikini, without baring any more flesh!

'Maybe later,' she said, turning away.

'Now.'

Bella frowned her irritation as she looked back at him. 'Gabriel, we don't have to literally bare all of ourselves to each other in the first few days of marriage!'

He gave a hard smile. 'You have seen *my* scars, now I would like to see yours.'

'I would rather not,' she came back crossly.

'Men and women all look alike in the daylight, too, Isabella,' Gabriel murmured throatily.

No, they didn't!

There was simply no other man like Gabriel. No

other man with his broodingly dark good looks. No other man with the power to make Bella's knees tremble with just a glance from the warmth of those chocolate-brown eyes. No other man who made her feel so desirable. No other man who could make her totally lose control at the merest touch of his hand…

There just was no other man as far as Bella was concerned.

Oh, God!

Bella felt her cheeks pale even as she stared up at Gabriel with a feeling of helplessness. She loved him. Loved Gabriel.

Had she *ever* really stopped loving him?

Probably not, Bella acknowledged with a feeling akin to panic. She had fallen in love with Gabriel that night five years ago, and even though she had never seen him again she had continued to love him.

That was the reason she had never been interested in even going out with another man for all these years.

That was the reason she had never felt even remotely attracted to another man in that time.

Because she was already in love with Gabriel Danti, and always would be!

And now she was married to him. Married to the man she loved, would always love, and yet could never tell him of that love because it wasn't what Gabriel wanted from her. It had never been what Gabriel wanted from her, and even less so now. All Gabriel wanted was his son; Bella just happened to come along with the package.

She stood up abruptly. 'I think not, thank you, Gabriel,' she told him stiffly. 'I'm tired. I'll go back to the villa and take a nap before dinner.'

Gabriel remained on the beach, his gaze narrowed in thought as he watched Bella walk into the trees and up towards the villa, her hair a black silky cloud down the slenderness of her back, the gentle sway of her hips wholly enticing.

What had happened just now?

One minute Bella had been challenging him as she always did, just as he had been enjoying that challenge as he always did, and the next it seemed she had completely shut down all her emotions.

Perhaps that was as well when Gabriel knew he daren't risk another pregnancy for Bella until he was sure she would be in no danger…

'Tell me what happened five years ago, Gabriel.'

'As in…?' Gabriel's expression was guarded as he looked across the dinner table at Bella.

'As in the accident, of course,' she said impatiently.

'Ah.' Gabriel sat back to take a sip of the white wine that he had opened to accompany the lobster and salad they had prepared together and just eaten.

Bella frowned. 'What did you think I meant?'

Gabriel looked at Bella beneath lowered lids as he admired her and thought how lovely she looked in her simple black knee-length gown. Its thin shoulder straps and the bareness of her arms revealed the light tan she had attained at the beach earlier, the heavy cloud of her dark hair cascaded loosely over that golden hue, and her face was bare of make-up except a pale peach lip gloss.

Bella had never looked more beautiful. Or more desirable.

'What did I think that you meant?' Gabriel repeated slowly. 'The night we spent together, perhaps?'

'I think we're both already well aware of what happened that night!' Bella pointed out tartly. 'Impressionable student meets sexy racing-car driver,' she enlarged as Gabriel raised questioning brows. 'And the rest is history, as they say!'

'What do *you* say, Bella?'

What should Bella say?

She could say that she had behaved like a complete idiot five years ago. She could say that she should have had more sense than to fall for all that rakish charm and spent that one glorious night in his arms. She could say that she should never have committed the complete folly of falling in love with a man like Gabriel Danti!

'Oh, no, you don't, Gabriel.' Her smile was tight. 'You're not going to distract me from my original question by annoying me.'

'I'm not?'

'No, you're not!'

He quirked dark brows. 'I am curious as to why our talking about the night we spent together five years ago should cause annoyance.'

'Gabriel!' she protested.

'Bella…?'

Maybe if he had continued to call her Isabella in that cold and distant way then Bella would have refused to answer him. Maybe. But when he said her name in that sexy, husky way she had no chance!

She sighed. 'I really don't want to argue with you again tonight, Gabriel.'

He nodded. 'Fine, then we will not argue.'

'We can't seem to do anything else!'

He shrugged his shoulders beneath the cream silk shirt he wore.

'We are here together for a week, Bella, with no other distractions. We have to talk about something.'

'I've already told you what happened that night. I'm more interested in what happened afterwards,' she said firmly.

Gabriel's mouth tightened. 'You are once again referring to the car crash in which two men died.'

The sudden coolness in his gaze, the slight withdrawal Bella sensed in his manner, told her how reluctant Gabriel was to talk about the accident.

At least as reluctant as Bella was to talk about that night they had spent together!

She gave him a direct look. 'I assure you I'm not going to be hurt by anything you have to say concerning your feelings for Janine Childe.'

'No?' Gabriel's eyes glittered in the moonlight that shone in the ever-encroaching darkness.

'No,' Bella said. 'You aren't the first man to go to bed with one woman when you're actually in love with another one. I very much doubt that you'll be the last, either!' she added with a rueful smile.

Gabriel's jaw tensed. 'You believe me so utterly dishonourable?'

'I believe you were a man surrounded by Formula One groupies who were only too happy to go to bed with defending champion Gabriel Danti, whether he was in love with someone else or not,' Bella explained practically.

'Formula One *groupies*?' Gabriel exclaimed.

'Oh, stop being obtuse, Gabriel,' Bella teased gently. 'Women of all ages find that macho image as sexy as hell, you know that.'

'Did you?' He sounded amused now.

'We weren't talking about *me*—'

'Why did you go to bed with me that night, Bella?'

He had called her Bella again! Her defences were already in tatters after the momentous recognition earlier of her love for this man, without that!

'Because you were sexy as hell, of course,' she said brightly. 'Now could you just—'

'Past tense, Bella?' Gabriel cut in softly, an edge to those husky tones. 'You no longer find me sexy?'

If Bella found Gabriel any sexier she would literally be drooling down her chin at how gorgeous he looked this evening with the dark thickness of his hair flowing onto his shoulders and the way that cream silk shirt emphasised every muscled inch of his chest.

If Bella found him any sexier she would be ripping that shirt from his back just so that she could touch bare flesh.

If she found Gabriel any sexier she would be on her knees begging him to make love to her again!

And again.

And again…

Just thinking about it made Bella's breasts firm and swell, the nipples hardening against the soft material of her dress, and an aching warmth begin to start between her thighs.

She shot him an irritated glance. 'You should have a public health warning stamped on your forehead!' She scowled as he began to smile. 'I'm glad *you* think it's funny,' she muttered.

Gabriel continued to smile as he regarded Bella across the width of the table. Without Bella realising it—or particularly wanting it?—they were becoming easier together in each other's company.

He sat forward slightly. 'Your public health warning should be on your breasts.'

Colour suffused Bella's cheeks. 'My *breasts*…?' she choked.

Gabriel nodded. 'They are beautiful, Bella. Firm. Round. A perfect fit in my hands. And your nipples are—'

'I'm not sure this is altogether polite after-dinner conversation, Gabriel!' she gasped when she could once more catch her breath.

Gabriel allowed his gaze to lower to the part of her anatomy under discussion as they pressed firm and pouting against the material of her gown. A clear indication that their conversation had roused Bella as much as it had him.

Yet he could not—no, he dared not—make love to her. The fear of further loss and trauma in his life made Gabriel determined not to put Bella's life at risk with a possible second pregnancy.

His mouth tightened as he realised the disastrous predicament he'd landed them both in. 'You are right, Isabella, it is not.' He stood up suddenly.

'I— Where are you going?' Bella frowned as Gabriel strode off towards the beach.

He turned on the pathway, the moonlight turning his hair to ebony and reflecting in his eyes. 'I require some time to myself,' he said distantly.

Gabriel needed some time to himself…

He couldn't have told Bella any more clearly that after only two days alone together he was already bored in her company!

'Fine.' She nodded abruptly. 'I'll see you in morning, then,' she added lamely, still slightly stunned by the way Gabriel's mood had changed so swiftly from seduction to a need to go off by himself. After spending so many weeks resisting him, Bella was also shocked by the fierce desire that she *wanted* to be seduced.

'No doubt,' he answered curtly.

And, Bella realised painfully, he looked far from pleased at the prospect...

The two days it had taken Gabriel to find himself bored with her company was the same two days it had taken Bella to realise she was more in love with him than ever!

CHAPTER TEN

'BREAKFAST, Bella.'

Bella felt as if she were fighting through layers of fog as she roused herself from a deep and troubled sleep, inwardly wincing as she remembered exactly where she was. And who she was with...

Once again Bella had pretended to be asleep the previous night when Gabriel had finally come to bed about two hours after her, and had known by the restlessness of Gabriel's movements as he lay beside her that he was no more asleep than she was.

Still they hadn't spoken. Hadn't touched. Had just lain there, side by side, awake but totally uncommunicative.

'Your coffee is becoming cold, Bella,' Gabriel told her sharply.

Bella could smell that coffee, and warm buttery croissants, finally opening her eyes to frown up at Gabriel as he stood beside the bed holding a breakfast tray. He was already fully dressed, his hair still damp from the shower, evidence that he had been up for some time.

'Why the breakfast in bed, Gabriel?' Bella sat up against the sumptuous pillows, having decided attack was her best form of defence after the way the two of them had parted the previous evening.

He shrugged. 'It seemed like something a new husband should do for his bride.' He placed the tray across her knees and stepped back.

'No one has ever brought me breakfast in bed before,' Bella muttered uncomfortably, keeping her gaze averted from him to instead look down at the pot of coffee and the freshly warmed croissants with a deliciously tempting pot of butter.

'As we are leaving later this morning I thought it best if I ensure you have something to eat—'

'Leaving?' Bella cut in incredulously, the breakfast tray forgotten as she stared up at Gabriel. 'As in going back to England leaving?'

He gave a haughty inclination of his head. 'As in going back to England leaving,' he confirmed evenly.

Bella was completely stunned as she watched Gabriel begin to take his clothes from the wardrobe obviously in preparation for packing them.

Gabriel had decided they were leaving. After only two days of their planned week-long honeymoon!

She gave a confused frown. 'This is all rather sudden, isn't it?'

What on earth were her family going to make of them cutting their honeymoon short like this? Especially Toby!

Gabriel saw the doubts flickering across Bella's face. A face that showed the strain of the last few days and nights in the heavy tiredness of her eyes and the unhappy slant to her mouth.

The same strain that Gabriel was feeling. Although he doubted that Bella's strain was for the same reason as his own!

He shook his head. 'You are unhappy here, Isabella.'

'So are you!' she shot back.

His mouth tightened. 'We were not talking about me.'

'No, we weren't, were we?' Bella said. 'Why is that, Gabriel? Why is it that you can never give me a straightforward answer to a straightforward question?'

Those dark eyes narrowed warningly. 'Perhaps because the questions you ask have no straightforward answer.'

She sighed in disgust. 'You're doing it again!'

Gabriel was well aware of what he was doing. But he could not tell Bella of his fears, of his need to leave here, before he once again put her life at risk if she conceived a second time. 'If you think that your family will be concerned at our early return from our honeymoon, then I suggest you go straight to your cottage. That way no one even has to know we are back.'

Bella frowned. 'What's the difference between us staying here for another five days or hiding out in my cottage?'

Gabriel gave a humourless smile. 'I said that *you* could go straight to your cottage, Isabella, not that I would be joining you there.'

Her face blanked of all expression. 'I see…'

'Do you?' Gabriel said grimly.

'Oh, yes,' Bella snapped as she placed the breakfast tray on the bedside table before swinging her legs to the floor and sitting up. 'I can be ready to leave in half an hour or so, if that's okay with you?'

Gabriel had thought Bella would be pleased at the idea

of leaving the island today. That she would be even happier at the idea of being relieved of his company once they were back in England. But instead she merely looked angry.

'There is no rush,' he told her. 'I have radioed ahead and instructed that the plane be fuelled and ready to leave as soon as we arrive.'

'Now I know where Toby gets his organisational skills from!' Bella huffed as she stood up. 'I would like some privacy to get showered and dressed, if you wouldn't mind, Gabriel?' She looked at him challengingly.

'Would it matter if I did?' he growled.

Her eyes flashed violet fire at him. 'Not in the least!'

His mouth thinned to a severe line. 'As I thought. Eat some of the breakfast, Isabella,' he instructed. 'You will feel less sick on the helicopter if you have eaten.'

'No—I'll just have something to be sick with!' she contradicted him mutinously.

'That is true, also,' Gabriel murmured dryly.

Bella glared. 'Please don't attempt to try and sugar-coat it for me!'

She looked so beautiful as she faced him across the room, her face flushed with anger and the darkness of her hair a wild tangle about her shoulders, the long, pale cream nightgown clinging to the lushness of her curvaceous figure.

It was all Gabriel could do to stop himself from taking the few steps that separated them before gathering Bella into his arms and making love to her until she screamed for mercy!

Instead he stepped towards the bedroom door. 'I will be outside if you should need me.'

'I won't,' she assured him firmly.

No, she probably wouldn't, Gabriel acknowledged ruefully as he strode outside into the sunshine to take deep, calming breaths of the fragrant air.

Much as he had done the previous evening as he walked along the moonlit shoreline and reminded himself all the reasons he dared not make love to Bella again…

'I thought you said you had to leave?' Bella reminded Gabriel many hours later as, having driven her to her cottage, he now lingered in the sitting-room.

The helicopter flight to the mainland had been less traumatic than the one going to the island, Bella having been prepared for the uneven flight this time.

The long flight on the Danti jet back to England had been free of incident, too—probably because neither of them had suggested going anywhere near the temptation of the bedroom at the back of the plane!

Once they'd landed in England Bella had protested the need for Gabriel to drive her back to the cottage. She could find her own way, she'd said. But it had been a battle she had lost. As she lost all of her battles against Gabriel…

But having been delivered here safely, Bella now expected him to leave. In fact, she was counting on it. Mainly because if Gabriel didn't soon go and leave her to her privacy, Bella knew she was going to give in to the hot tears that had been threatening to fall all day!

'Are you not going to at least offer me a cup of coffee?' Gabriel asked.

Her eyes widened. 'It's late, Gabriel, and I thought you had somewhere else to go.'

He frowned. 'I did not say that.'

'You implied it.'

Gabriel was well aware of what he had implied. As he was aware, now the time had come to part from Bella, that he was reluctant to do so.

'I am not sure it is the right thing to do, to just leave you here on your own.'

She laughed humourlessly. 'I've lived on my own for two years, Gabriel—'

'You have lived here with Toby,' he cut in firmly. 'That is not the same thing.'

No, it wasn't, Bella accepted ruefully, already aware of how quiet, how empty, the cottage seemed without her small son's presence.

'I'm a big girl now, Gabriel; I'm sure I'll manage,' she said dryly.

His eyes darkened in intensity, that familiar nerve pulsing in his clenched jaw. 'I am well aware of the fact that you are a big girl, Isabella.'

'Then I suggest you stop treating me like I'm six years old rather than twenty-six!'

His mouth flattened into a disapproving line. 'Showing concern for your welfare is treating you like a child?'

Bella shook her head impatiently. 'No, actually treating me like a child is doing that!'

'How would you have me treat you, Isabella?' Gabriel glowered his frustration with this conversation.

Bella became very still, very aware of the sudden tension in the room. She could almost feel the crackle of electricity that arced between herself and Gabriel…

She swallowed hard. 'I think you should just go.'

Gabriel thought so, too. In fact, he knew so! Before

he did something he would later regret. Something they might both have reason to regret.

Except…

Bella looked tired after their long journey, her eyes purple smudges in a face that was pale with exhaustion, and the fullness of her lips bare of lip gloss. But nevertheless there was a beguiling determination to the stubborn lift of her chin, that challenge reflected in the brilliance of her eyes and the proud stance of her tiny body.

Gabriel felt the throb of his arousal just looking at her. Telling him it was definitely time that he left!

'I should go, yes,' he acknowledged huskily.

'Yes.'

'Now.'

'Yes.'

'Bella—'

'Gabriel…?'

He drew in a ragged breath. 'I need to go!'

'You do.'

Except Gabriel moved *towards* Bella rather than away from her as he crossed the room in two long strides to pull her hard against him even as his head lowered and his mouth claimed hers in a need as primitive and as old as time.

As wild and primitive as his fierce, uncontrollable desire to possess Bella again…

Gabriel's hands moved to become entangled in her hair as he kissed her hungrily, fiercely, his lips parting hers and allowing his tongue to plunge deeply into the heat beyond. Bella's mouth tasted of honey, and was hot, so very hot, as she drew him deeper inside her.

Gabriel curved her body into the hardness of his as he continued to kiss and claim her. His hands spread over her bottom as he pulled her against him and pressed her to the ache in his thighs, his arousal hard and pulsing, demanding, the need to possess her so strong that Gabriel could think of nothing else, feel nothing else but Bella.

He wrenched his mouth from hers to bury his face against the satin smoothness of her throat, licking, tasting, biting. 'We should stop this now, Bella!'

'Yes,' she breathed shakily.

'I cannot be gentle with you!' Gabriel groaned, knowing it was true. He had waited too long. Wanted her for far too long!

Bella already knew that, had felt his urgency the moment he took her in his arms. An urgency that she echoed, that had ignited the moment he'd touched her. No, even before he'd touched her! This physical awareness had been there between them all day, Bella realised now, burning just below the surface of even the most mundane of conversations.

'I won't break, Gabriel,' she encouraged, her throat arched to the erotic heat of his questing mouth, her fingers entangled in the silky softness of his hair. 'Just don't stop. Please don't stop...' She quivered with longing, several buttons ripping off her blouse as Gabriel parted it to bare her breasts to his lips and tongue, drawing one swollen tip into the heat of his mouth hungrily as one of his hands cupped and squeezed its twin.

Bella sobbed low in her throat as the pleasure ripped through her, to become centred as a hot ache between her thighs. She was so swollen there, so needy as she pressed against Gabriel's arousal, she could barely think straight.

He moved against her, his hardness, his length and thickness, a promise of even greater pleasure. A pleasure Bella had no intention of letting Gabriel deny either of them. She wanted him inside her. Wanted to look up at Gabriel, to watch his face as he stroked long and hard inside her. Wanted to hear his groans of pleasure as they matched her own. To hear his cries as they reached that pinnacle together.

'Not this time, Gabriel.' She moved away as his hand went to open the fastening of her jeans. 'I want to touch you first. Kiss you. All of you,' she added huskily, her gaze deliberately holding his as she unbuttoned his shirt before slowly slipping it down his arms and dropping it onto the carpeted floor. Her fingers looked much paler than the darkness of Gabriel's skin as she touched the hard wall of his chest. 'You're so beautiful, Gabriel…!' she whispered before she began to kiss each and every one of his scars, her tongue a delicate rasp against the heat of his skin as she tasted him.

Gabriel knew that his scarred body was far from beautiful, but he ceased to care about anything else as Bella's lips roamed across him freely, her tongue flickering against him even as her hand flattened against the hardness of his arousal, his erection responding immediately as that hand moved against him slowly, rhythmically. Gabriel felt his blood pulsing, pounding, increasing in urgency.

They had spent five weeks together before their wedding and two days alone on a romantic Caribbean island. And yet it was here, and now, in Bella's tiny cottage, when he knew they would be apart for several hours, that Gabriel completely lost control!

'I need—Bella, I need—' He broke off with a groan as Bella unfastened his jeans and pushed them out of the way so that she might fulfil that need.

Her mouth was so hot as she took him inside her, her tongue moist and her fingers curling about him as she caressed the length of him.

Gabriel became lost in the pleasure of this dual assault upon his senses, his neck arched, his muscles tensing, locking, as he fought to maintain control.

Just a little longer. He wanted—needed to enjoy being with Bella just a little longer, and then he would leave, Gabriel promised himself silently as Bella manoeuvred him gently backwards so that he sat down in an armchair, her hair a wild tumble about his thighs as she knelt in front of him.

Just a few minutes more of being inside the heat of Bella's mouth. Of her wicked little tongue moistly caressing the length of his shaft. Of her fingers about him as he instinctively began to move to that same mind-blowing rhythm.

Bella raised her lids to look at Gabriel, deliberately holding his gaze with hers as her tongue swirled provocatively about the head of his pulsing erection. Licking. Teasing. Tasting.

Gabriel's face was flushed with arousal, his eyes fevered, his jaw clenched, and the muscles standing out in his throat as he fought not to lose that control.

'No more!' he growled even as he reached down and pulled Bella away from him, grasping her arms to lift her up so that his mouth could capture hers. Bella straddled him as they kissed wildly, feverishly, Gabriel's hands hot against her back as his mouth made love to hers.

Gabriel stood up, their mouths still fused wildly together. His hands cupped about Bella's bottom to lift her up with him before he lay her down on the carpeted floor, lifting his head to part her already ruined blouse and then feast on her naked breasts.

He kissed first one nipple and then the other, Bella whimpering softly when he finally raised his head to look down at the swollen fullness of her breasts. His gaze deliberately held hers as he moved to his knees beside her to brush the pads of his thumbs over those achingly sensitive nipples, watching the way Bella's eyes darkened and she groaned low in her throat even as she arched up into that caress.

Gabriel continued to hold that gaze as he unfastened her jeans and peeled them down her thighs to remove them completely, parting her legs so that he could move in between them. His hands were big and dark against her abdomen as he caressed her in slow swirling movements in a deliberate path to the soft, dark curls that were visible to him through the cream lace of her panties.

Bella was breathing hard as she watched Gabriel touching her, his fingers warm and gentle. A low moan escaped her as he swept one of those fingers against the lacy material that covered the cleft between her legs, her hips moving up to meet that tantalising caress.

That finger moved against her again.

Again Bella moved up to meet that caress.

And again.

Teasing her. Pleasuring her. Torturing her.

'Yes, Gabriel…!' Bella finally pleaded as she moved against him in frustration.

He peeled her panties down her thighs and legs to discard them completely, his eyes intense as he looked down at her before slowly lowering his head. First his hands touched her, then his lips, softly, tenderly as he kissed the scar that hadn't been there five years ago.

But Bella had no time to dwell on that as his fingers parted the dark curls beneath and his mouth moved lower…

Dear God!

Pleasure unlike anything she had ever known before radiated out to every part of her body as the sweep of Gabriel's tongue against that pulsing nub brought her to the edge of release and then took her crashing over it in wave after wave of such intensity it was almost pain.

Bella was mindless with pleasure, her breath releasing in a sob as she felt Gabriel part her sensitive folds and enter her, first with one finger, and then with two. As his tongue continued to caress that aching nub her head moved wildly from side to side and her hands clenched as Gabriel took her to a climax that was even more intense than the first.

It wasn't enough.

It would never be enough!

Bella surged up to push Gabriel down onto the carpet and pull off his remaining clothes before moving up and over him, her hands resting against his shoulders as the heat between her thighs became a hot caress against the hardness of his shaft, her breasts a temptation just beyond his reach as she bent slightly towards him.

'No, Bella—' Gabriel broke off with a groan as she opened herself to him and took him into her, inch by slow inch, until he was completely inside her. Her heat, her tightness wrapped around him. 'We must not do this—'

'*I* must,' she insisted.

Gabriel ceased breathing altogether as Bella began to move with an agonising slowness that sent the pleasure rocketing into his brain and down to his toes.

Gabriel felt himself grow even harder, bigger, no longer able to bear the torment of her breasts above him as he moved his head up and captured one of those rose-tipped breasts into his mouth.

Bella plunged down to take him deeper, before moving up so that only the very tip of him remained inside her. Before plunging down again and again. Gabriel was so big now, so long that it felt as if he touched the very centre of her.

His hands moved to grasp her hips and guide her movements as he felt his imminent release, hearing Bella's cry as she reached a climax at the same time as he did.

CHAPTER ELEVEN

'WE SHOULD not have done that!'

Bella had collapsed weakly against the dampness of Gabriel's chest as the last of the pleasure rippled through her body, but she raised her head now to look down at him incredulously. '*What* did you just say?'

Gabriel's expression was grim as he returned her gaze. 'I should not have done this, Bella—'

She gasped in shock, moving abruptly back and then away from him, clasping her ruined blouse about her nakedness as she disengaged their bodies before standing up. 'Get out, Gabriel,' she choked.

'Bella—'

'Just *get out*!' she repeated shakily, turning away to find her panties, her legs trembling slightly as she tried to balance before pulling them on over her nakedness.

How could Gabriel do this to her? How could he?

What she had thought of as being something beautiful, utterly unique, had now become nothing more than something she wished to forget.

To wish had never happened!

'Would you just put some clothes on and leave, Gabriel?'

He rose slowly to his feet, magnificent in his nakedness, his hair tousled about his shoulders, his chest broad and muscled, thighs powerful still, his legs long and elegant.

Bella turned away from looking at all that raw, male beauty. 'I don't want you to say anything, Gabriel. I don't want you to do anything. I just want you to get dressed and leave. Now,' she insisted.

'Bella—'

'*Now!*'

'You misunderstood my reasoning just now, Bella—'

'Don't touch me!' She moved sharply away from the hands he placed on her shoulders, shying away from even that physical contact.

Gabriel frowned fiercely as he saw her expression. 'You did not seem to find my touch so distasteful a few minutes ago,' he rasped.

'Any more than you did mine,' she retaliated. 'I guess we both just got so carried away with the moment we forgot to look at the broader picture!'

Gabriel's eyes narrowed. 'And what might that be?' he asked softly.

'Will you just get some clothes on?' she repeated impatiently. 'I find it a little disconcerting talking to a man when he's completely naked.'

'I'm not just any man, Isabella, I am your husband,' he pointed out harshly as he swiftly pulled his jeans back on and fastened them.

'I know exactly who and what you are, Gabriel,' she said. 'What I meant, Gabriel, is that the only reason you married me was because of Toby—'

'Isabella—'

'Would you have even thought of offering me marriage if not for Toby?' she challenged.

'Neither of us will ever know now what would have happened after we met again in San Francisco—'

'*I* know,' Bella said scornfully. 'I very much doubt we would ever have seen each other again after San Francisco if you hadn't learnt of Toby's existence!'

Gabriel drew in a deep, controlling breath. 'This is perhaps not the time to talk about this. You are distraught—'

'I'm *angry*, Gabriel, not distraught. With myself,' she added. 'For falling—yet again!—for your seduction routine!'

'My seduction routine?' he echoed incredulously.

Bella nodded. 'No doubt honed over years spent on the Formula One racing circuit! And don't bother trying to deny it,' she warned. 'I still remember the practised way you seduced me five years ago!'

He scowled. 'That was five years ago, Isabella—'

'Then you must be pleased to know that you haven't lost any of your seductive skills!' she snapped.

Gabriel studied her closely, wanting to take her in his arms, to explain his fears for her—

'Insulting me is only making this situation worse, Bella,' he told her softly instead.

'Worse? Could it be any worse?' she cried. 'We've just ripped each other's clothes off in a sexual frenzy—in my case, literally.' She looked down at her gaping blouse, the buttons scattered on the carpet at their feet. 'I don't want to talk about this any more, Gabriel,' she told him flatly, her expression bleak. 'All I want is for you to leave.'

Gabriel's mouth firmed. 'I will return tomorrow—'

'Don't hurry back on my account!' she exclaimed.

'We need to talk.'

'I very much doubt that there's anything you have to say that I will want to hear,' she told him wearily.

A nerve pulsed in Gabriel's clenched jaw. Bella looked so beautiful with the darkness of her hair tangled about her shoulders, and her lips still swollen from the heat of their kisses, so utterly desirable, that all Gabriel wanted was to take her in his arms and make love with her again. And again.

'Nevertheless, I will return later tomorrow,' he bit out with grim determination.

She raised mocking brows as he made no effort to leave. 'I hope you aren't waiting for me to tell you I'll be looking forward to it!'

'No, I am not expecting you to say that.' Gabriel gave a humourless smile. 'Your honesty is one of the things I like most about you, Bella.'

'One of the few things, I'm sure,' she said knowingly. 'If you'll excuse me, now?' She turned away. 'I would like to take a shower and then go to bed.'

Alone, Bella could have added, but didn't. What was the point in stating the obvious?

She raised her chin defensively. 'Goodbye, Gabriel.'

'It will never be goodbye between the two of us, Isabella,' he stated calmly.

No, it never would be, Bella accepted heavily once Gabriel had finally gone. They would continue with this sham of a marriage for as long as it took. For as long as Toby needed them to do so.

For Toby...

Her small, happily contented son had absolutely no

idea that his very existence had condemned his parents to a marriage that was completely devoid of love.

Except Bella's love for Gabriel.

A love she would never—could never, reveal to him…

'Where have you been?'

'Where does it look as if I've been?' Bella answered Gabriel sarcastically as she carried on taking the bags of shopping from the boot of her car. 'I wasn't expecting you back just yet,' she added as Gabriel took some of those bags out of her hands.

She had seen the powerful black sports car parked outside the cottage as soon as she turned her own car down the lane, a heaviness settling in her chest as she easily recognised Gabriel sitting behind the wheel.

Despite her exhaustion Bella had lain awake in bed for hours the previous night, unable to stop thinking about Gabriel. About the wild ecstasy of their lovemaking. And then of his declaration that they shouldn't have made love at all…!

Consequently it had been almost dawn before she had finally fallen asleep. Almost midday before she'd woke up again, feeling as if she hadn't slept at all. Several hours, and half a dozen cups of black coffee later, before she'd summoned up the energy to dress and go out to shop for food.

Which was where she had obviously been when Gabriel had arrived at the cottage. Much earlier than she had expected—it was only a little after five o'clock—and looking much too rakishly handsome for Bella's comfort in a black polo shirt and faded jeans.

'Thanks,' Bella accepted coolly as he carried half a

dozen of the bags through to the kitchen for her. 'Can I get you a coffee or anything?' she said offhandedly, her face averted as she began to unpack the bags.

But—as usual!—she was still very much aware of Gabriel as he stood only a couple of feet away from her as she put the groceries away in the cupboards. Silently. Watchfully.

'Better yet,' she added brightly, 'why don't you make yourself useful and prepare the coffee while I finish putting these things away? Gabriel…?' she said uncertainly when he didn't answer her. In fact, Bella realised with a frown, he hadn't said a word since asking where she had been…

Gabriel looked at her quizzically, easily noting the dark shadows beneath her eyes, and the hollows of her cheeks, the pallor of her face thrown into stark relief by the fact that her hair was drawn back and secured at her crown with a toothed clasp.

Dressed in a deep pink T-shirt that clung to the fullness of her breasts, and jeans that emphasised the slenderness of her hips and legs, and with her face completely bare of make-up, Bella looked ten years younger than the twenty-six years she had only yesterday evening assured him she actually was.

Gabriel's mouth tightened as he thought of yesterday evening. 'I will make the coffee. Then I wish for the two of us to talk.'

She stiffened. 'Not about last night, I hope?'

He gave a stiff inclination of his head. 'Amongst other things.'

Bella made a movement of denial. 'There's nothing left for us to say about last night—'

'There is *everything* for us to say about last night!' Gabriel contradicted her furiously before visibly controlling himself. 'I will not let you put even more barriers between us, Bella. If you prefer, I will talk, and you need only listen…?'

Bella eyed him warily, having no idea what he could have to say that she would want to listen to. He had said far too much last night!

'And if I don't like what you have to say?' she challenged.

'Then I will have to respect that,' he said curtly.

Bella continued to look at him wordlessly for several long seconds before giving an abrupt nod of her head. 'Fine,' she said. 'Just make the coffee first, hmm?'

What should have been a relaxed domestic scene, with Bella putting the groceries away and Gabriel making the pot of coffee, was anything but! Bella was far too aware of Gabriel—on every level—to feel in the least relaxed.

How could she possibly relax when Gabriel was just too vibrantly male? Too ruggedly handsome. Too physically overpowering. Too—too everything!

But, having finally put all the shopping away, two mugs of hot coffee poured and Gabriel already seated at the kitchen table, there was nothing else Bella could do to delay sitting down and listening while Gabriel talked.

'Well?' she prompted sharply after several seconds, the silence between them so absolute that Bella could hear every tick of the clock hanging on the wall above the dresser.

Gabriel's expression was pained. 'I realise you are still angry with me, Bella, but I do not believe I have done anything to deserve your contempt.'

Not recently, Bella acknowledged self-derisively, having accepted during her deliberations last night that she was just as responsible for what had happened between them the previous evening as Gabriel was. That she had wanted him as much as he had appeared to want her.

She sighed heavily. 'I'm not angry, Gabriel,' she admitted ruefully. 'At least, not with you.'

He gave her a searching glance. 'You are angry with yourself because we made love last night?'

'We had *sex* last night, Gabriel—'

'We *made love*—'

'You can call it what you like, but we both know what it really was!' Her eyes glittered angrily.

Gabriel drew in another controlling breath. 'I thought I was going to talk and you were going to listen?'

'Not if you're going to say things I don't agree with!' she snapped.

Gabriel didn't know whether to shake Bella or kiss her! Although he very much doubted that Bella would welcome either action in her present mood.

'I will endeavour not to do so,' he teased.

'You just can't guarantee it,' Bella acknowledged dryly.

Gabriel shrugged. 'It is not always possible to know what is or is not going to anger you.'

'Well, as long as you steer clear of last night or anything that happened five years ago, you should be on pretty safe ground!'

Gabriel grimaced. 'Ah.'

Her eyes widened. 'You *are* going to tell me about five years ago…?'

'It was my intention to do so, yes.'

'But—you've never wanted to talk about it!'

'The situation has changed— Bella…?' he questioned as she stood up abruptly and moved to stand with her back to the room as she stared out of the kitchen window.

Bella's neck was so delicately vulnerable, her back slender, her shoulders narrow—far too narrow, Gabriel acknowledged heavily, for her to have carried alone the burden of her pregnancy and then the bringing up of their son for the last four and a half years.

'Please, Bella…?' he asked again softly.

It felt as if Bella's heart were actually being squeezed in her chest as she heard the gentleness in Gabriel's tone.

When they were on the island she had asked Gabriel to tell her what really happened five years ago. At the time she had genuinely wanted to know the answer. But now—now when Bella already felt so vulnerable and exposed by her realised love for him, by the wildness of their lovemaking the previous evening— she really wasn't sure she could bear to hear Gabriel talk about his feelings for another woman.

Especially if he were to tell her he still had those feelings for Janine Childe…!

Coward, a little voice inside her head taunted mockingly. Bella had always known that Gabriel hadn't, didn't, and never would love her, so what difference did it make if he was now willing to talk about five years ago?

It shouldn't matter at all!

But it did…

Bella stiffened her shoulders, her expression deliberately unreadable as she turned back to face Gabriel. A defensive stance that almost crumbled as the gentleness she had heard in Gabriel's tone was echoed in the darkness of his eyes as he looked across the kitchen at her.

Damn it, she didn't want his pity!

She wanted his love. She had wanted that five years ago, and she wanted it even more now. But if she couldn't have that then she certainly didn't want his pity!

Her shoulders straightened and her chin raised in challenge. 'Go ahead,' she finally invited tightly.

Gabriel continued to look at her silently for several seconds, and then he gave a decisive inclination of his head. 'First I need to tell you where I have been since we parted yesterday evening—'

'You said we were going to talk about what happened five years ago!' Bella cut in impatiently. Having built herself up, having placed a shield about her shaky emotions, Bella now needed to get this conversation over with before that barrier crumbled into dust!

Gabriel sighed at the interruption. 'My actions since we parted yesterday are relevant to that past. Sit with me, Bella?' Gabriel encouraged huskily as he saw that her face was paler than ever, those dark shadows beneath her eyes emphasised further by that pallor.

The fact that Bella actually did as he asked told Gabriel how much his presence, this conversation, had unsettled her. The last thing he wanted to do was hurt Bella any more than he already had, and yet it seemed his mere presence had managed do that.

He rubbed his eyes wearily. 'I will leave any time you ask me to do so, Bella.'

She gave a humourless smile. 'Is that a promise?'

'If you wish it, yes,' Gabriel assured her wryly.

Her eyed widened at his compliance. 'Are you sure you haven't received a blow to the head while you've been away?'

'Very funny, Bella,' he drawled.

'One tries,' she teased lightly.

Gabriel wasn't fooled for a moment by Bella's attempt at levity, knew by the wariness in her eyes and the tension beside her mouth that it was only a façade.

As his own calm was only a façade.

A nerve pulsed beside the livid scar on Gabriel's cheek. 'Bella, when we were on the island you asked me what really happened five years ago, when three Formula One cars crashed and two other men were killed as a consequence. Do you still want to know the answer to that question?'

'Yes, of course!'

'And you will believe me if I tell you the truth?'

'Of course I'll believe you, Gabriel.' She looked irritated that he should doubt it.

He smiled briefly. 'As was stated at the time, the findings of the official enquiry were that it was a complete accident, but I knew—I have always known—that it was Paulo Descari, and not I, who was responsible for our three cars colliding.'

'But—' Bella gasped. 'It was deliberate?'

Gabriel's jaw clenched. 'I believe so, yes.'

Bella stared at him, her expression once again blank. Why on earth would Paulo Descari have done such a thing? Unless...

'Because Janine Childe had decided she had made a

mistake? That she returned your love, after all?' Bella realised heavily. 'Had she told Paulo Descari she was ending their relationship in order to come back to you?'

Gabriel's expression was grim as he stood up abruptly. 'Neither of those things was possible, I am afraid, Bella,' he rasped. 'The first for the simple reason that there was no love on my side for Janine Childe to return. The second because it was I who had ended our brief relationship, and not the other way around as Janine so publicly claimed only hours after the accident. But I do believe Janine may have taunted Paulo with our relationship,' he continued. 'He tried to provoke an argument with me that morning, was so blind with jealousy that he would not believe me when I told him I had no feelings for Janine.' He sighed heavily. 'I was not physically responsible for the accident, Bella, but I have nevertheless always felt a certain guilt, not only because of my complete indifference to Janine, but because I survived and two other men did not.'

'But that's— You have no reason to feel guilty, Gabriel.' Bella gasped. 'You could so easily have died, too!'

'And instead I am here. With you,' Gabriel murmured huskily.

How long would it take for Bella to realise, to question, after the things he had just told her, the night the two of them had spent together five years ago?

Gabriel watched as the blankness left Bella's face to be replaced with a frown, that frown disappearing, too, seconds later as she looked across at him questioningly.

Gabriel drew in a controlling breath. 'I was unconscious for several days after the accident, and so was unable at the time to deny or confirm Janine's claim that I had caused the accident because I was still in love with her.' His top lip turned back contemptuously. 'By the time I was well enough to deny her accusations I simply did not care to do so,' he added flatly.

'Why didn't you?' Bella demanded incredulously. 'Surely you must have realised that Janine Childe's claims gave people reason to continue to have doubts despite the findings of the official enquiry?'

His eyes narrowed. 'Did you have reason to continue to doubt them, too, Bella?'

She shook her head vehemently. 'Not over your innocence, no.'

Gabriel had thought, had hoped this would be easier than it was. But it wasn't. Baring his soul in this way, with no idea of the outcome, was excruciating.

'I don't understand why you didn't speak out, Gabriel,' Bella said. 'From what you've said, you were supposed to be the one who died that day!'

He turned away. 'Jason was dead. As was Paulo. When people die, Bella, all that is left is the memories people who loved them have of them. What good did it do anyone, but especially Paulo and Jason's families, for me to claim that one man had possibly been deliberately responsible for the death of the other?'

Bella could see the logic behind Gabriel's words—she just couldn't make any sense of it!

'That was…very self-sacrificing, of you,' she murmured gently.

'More so than even I realised,' he acknowledged harshly.

She looked up sharply as a realisation hit her. 'You

really didn't make love to me that night because you were upset at losing Janine Childe to another man, did you?'

His smile was rueful. 'No, I did not.'

'Then—that morning you—' She moistened dry lips. 'You said you would call me. Did you really mean it?'

'Yes.'

'You did?' The beat of Bella's heart sounded very loud in her ears as her thoughts—her hopes, rose wildly.

'I did,' Gabriel confirmed heavily. 'Our night together had been—surprising.'

'Really?'

'Yes.' Gabriel took a deep breath. 'Unfortunately that altercation with Paulo meant I did not have chance to ring you before the practice session, and obviously I was unable to do so afterwards. Then, once I recovered and there had been no word from you, I believed you did not want to know.'

Bella's hands were clenched so tightly that she could feel her nails piercing the skin of her palms. Gabriel hadn't been in love with Janine Childe, not then and certainly not now. Gabriel had meant it that morning five years ago when he had said he would call her.

Tears blurred Bella's vision, Gabriel just a hazy outline as he stood so still and silent across the kitchen. 'I thought—I didn't believe I would ever see you again after that night.'

'A belief that became fact,' Gabriel rasped.

'But not because you wanted it that way!' Bella protested achingly.

'No.'

'Gabriel, I—I don't know what to say!' She stood up

restlessly. 'I was sitting at home that night when the announcement of the crash came on the evening news. Saw the two bodies lying on the ground. You being carried away on a stretcher before they placed you in the ambulance and rushed you off to hospital. It was the worst moment of my life.' She gave a disbelieving shake of her head. 'Or, at least, I thought it was, until Janine Childe appeared on the television immediately afterwards claiming that you were still in love with her.'

'It never occurred to me—I never realised that her lies would have convinced anyone, but I suppose I knew the real Janine, and you didn't." Gabriel frowned.

'It was the one about your being in love with her that I thought to be true,' Bella admitted. 'I didn't know you well, Gabriel, but I certainly never believed you capable of deliberately harming another man.'

'Bella, what would you have done that day if you had not believed I was in love with Janine?'

'I would have come to you, of course!' she exclaimed. 'I wouldn't have cared who had tried to stop me. I would have made them let me see you!'

'Why?'

Bella raised wary eyes to his. 'Why…?'

'Why, Bella?' Gabriel repeated gruffly.

Because she had fallen in love with him that night, that was why! Because she was still in love with him!

Gabriel's eyes narrowed as he saw the uncertainty flicker across Bella's face. The wariness. The desire not to be hurt again.

Gabriel felt that same desire, both five years ago and again now.

He drew in a deep breath, accepting that one of them

had to break the deadlock between them. 'Perhaps if I were to tell you why it was that I had no interest in what people believed happened that day…?'

Bella blinked, her throat moving convulsively as she swallowed hard before speaking. 'Why didn't you, Gabriel?'

His mouth twisted. 'For the same reason that nothing mattered to me when I regained consciousness two days after the accident.' He shrugged. 'Because you were not there, Bella,' he admitted bluntly. 'You were not there. Had never been there. And no matter how much I wished for it during those three months I spent in hospital, you still did not come.'

Bella looked totally stunned now. 'I don't understand…'

'No, I do not suppose that you do,' he accepted ruefully as he was the one to take the two steps that separated them before raising one of his hands to curve it about the coolness of her cheek. 'My beautiful Bella. My brave beautiful Bella.' He smiled emotionally. 'After all this time, all you have suffered, you deserve to know the truth.'

'The truth…?'

'That I fell in love with you that night five years ago—'

'No…!' Her cry was agonised and Gabriel only just managed to prevent her from falling as her knees gave way beneath her.

'Yes, Bella.' Gabriel's arms moved about her, his cheek resting against the darkness of her hair as he gathered her close against his chest. 'Impossible as it must seem, I fell in love with you that night. I have loved you always, Bella. You and only you. So much so that there has been no other woman in my life, or my bed, these last five years,' he added gruffly.

Bella clung to him as his words washed over and then into her. She had been stunned by what he had told her about the accident and by Janine Childe's duplicity, but this was even more shocking.

Gabriel loved her. He had always loved her.

The tears fell hotly down Bella's cheeks as she clung to him.

As she cried for all the pain and disillusionment they had unwittingly caused each other through misunderstandings. For all the time they had wasted…

She pulled away from him slightly before looking up into his face, her heart aching as she still saw the uncertainty in his face. 'Gabriel, impossible as it must seem, I fell in love with you that night five years ago, too.' Bella held his gaze with hers as she deliberately repeated his words. 'I have loved you always, Gabriel. You and only you. So much so that there has been no other man in my life, or my bed, these last five years.'

His expression didn't change. He didn't blink. He didn't speak. He didn't even seem to be breathing as he continued to stare down at her.

'Gabriel?' Bella's gaze searched his face worriedly. 'Gabriel, I love you. I love you!' she repeated desperately as she reached up to clasp his arms and shake him slightly. 'I never meant to let you down after the accident, I just thought I had been a one-night stand to you. Gabriel, please—'

'You did not let me down, Bella,' he cut in harshly. 'You have never let me down. *I* was the one who let *you* down when it did not even occur to me that you might believe I was in love with Janine. *I* was the one who let *you* down by not even thinking you might become pregnant from our night together. How can you love me after what you have suffered because my pride would not let me be the one to seek you out again? How can you love me when my arrogance, my intolerance, meant you had to go through your pregnancy, Toby's birth, the first four and a half years of his life, completely alone?'

'Gabriel, I'd really rather you didn't continue to insult the man I love,' Bella interrupted shakily. 'And I wasn't alone,' she reassured him. 'I had my parents. My sister and brother.'

'I should have been there for you, too,' Gabriel growled in self-disgust. 'Instead of which, when we did finally meet up again, I only made matters worse by forcing you into marrying me.' He shook his head. 'I should not have done that, Bella.'

'You're Toby's father—'

'He was not the reason I forced our marriage upon you, Bella. It was—' He stopped and then sighed. 'Having met you again, having realised that I still love you, I could not bear the thought of having to let you go again!'

Gabriel hadn't married her just for Toby, after all?

Bella looked puzzled. 'But if you felt that way—if you do still love me—'

'I love you now more than ever, Bella,' he assured her fiercely.

'Then why did we leave the island so abruptly?'

'We left the island so suddenly for the same reason I should not have allowed our lovemaking last night to go as far as it did,' Gabriel cut in grimly. 'You almost died giving birth to Toby, Bella. I would not—I did not want to put your life at risk by another unplanned pregnancy, and so I decided we had to leave the island before I gave in to the temptation being alone there with you represented. That we needed to consult an obstetrician before we made love again. Instead of which, as soon as we were back here, I allowed—!' He shook his head. 'I had an appointment to see a specialist in Harley Street today, needed to know that a second pregnancy would not endanger your life. He was most unhelpful,' Gabriel said, patently annoyed, 'and said he could not pass comment before first examining you.'

'You spoke to an obstetrician about me...?' Bella echoed dazedly.

Gabriel frowned darkly. 'What if you are pregnant right now, Bella?' His face had gone pale at the mere thought of it. 'What if our time together last night results in another child?'

A slow, beatific smile curved Bella's lips as she realised their sudden flight from the island, Gabriel's grimness after they made love last night, had all been for one reason and one reason only.

'Then I, for one, would be absolutely thrilled,' she assured him breathlessly. 'I thought you wanted lots of brothers and sisters for Toby?' she cajoled as Gabriel still looked haunted.

'Not at the risk of losing you,' he stated definitely.

'We don't know for sure that there is any risk,' Bella teased him, no longer daunted by the fierceness of Gabriel's moods. He loved her. They loved each other. Together they could overcome any obstacles that might come their way.

'Until you have seen this obstetrician we do not know for sure that there is not, either,' Gabriel persisted.

'Have a little faith, Gabriel. Remember you're a Danti!'

Some of the tension started to leave Gabriel's body as Bella's eyes laughed up into his. 'Are you mocking me, Bella?'

'Just a little.' Her throaty chuckle gave lie to the claim. 'I'm all for taking risks, Gabriel. In fact, I think a little more risk-taking right now might be good for both of us…' she added huskily, taking his hand in hers to begin walking towards the stairs, shooting him a provocative smile over her shoulder as she did so.

Gabriel followed Bella like a man in a daze, totally unable to deny her anything. Knowing that he never would be able to deny her anything. That, having found her again, knowing she loved him as much as he loved her, that she always had, he intended spending the rest of his life loving as well as protecting Bella.

Their daughter, Clara Louisa, was born safely and without complications exactly a year later, followed two years later by the equally safe birth of their twin sons, Simon Henry and Peter Cristo…

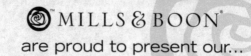

millsandboon.co.uk Community

Join Us!

The Community is the perfect place to meet and chat to kindred spirits who love books and reading as much as you do, but it's also the place to:

- Get the inside scoop from authors about their latest books
- Learn how to write a romance book with advice from our editors
- Help us to continue publishing the best in women's fiction
- Share your thoughts on the books we publish
- Befriend other users

Forums: Interact with each other as well as authors, editors and a whole host of other users worldwide.

Blogs: Every registered community member has their own blog to tell the world what they're up to and what's on their mind.

Book Challenge: We're aiming to read 5,000 books and have joined forces with The Reading Agency in our inaugural Book Challenge.

Profile Page: Showcase yourself and keep a record of your recent community activity.

Social Networking: We've added buttons at the end of every post to share via digg, Facebook, Google, Yahoo, technorati and de.licio.us.

www.millsandboon.co.uk

2 FREE BOOKS
AND A SURPRISE GIFT

We would like to take this opportunity to thank you for reading this
Mills & Boon® book by offering you the chance to take TWO more
specially selected books from the Modern™ series absolutely FREE!
We're also making this offer to introduce you to the benefits of the
Mills & Boon® Book Club™—

- **FREE home delivery**
- **FREE gifts and competitions**
- **FREE monthly Newsletter**
- **Exclusive Mills & Boon Book Club offers**
- **Books available before they're in the shops**

Accepting these FREE books and gift places you under no obligation to buy, you may cancel at any time, even after receiving your free
books. Simply complete your details below and return the entire page
to the address below. You don't even need a stamp!

YES Please send me 2 free Modern books and a surprise gift. I
understand that unless you hear from me, I will receive 4 superb new
books every month for just £3.19 each, postage and packing free. I
am under no obligation to purchase any books and may cancel my
subscription at any time. The free books and gift will be mine to keep
in any case.

Ms/Mrs/Miss/Mr_____ Initials _____

Surname _____
Address _____

_____ Postcode _____

Send this whole page to: Mills & Boon Book Club, Free Book Offer,
FREEPOST NAT 10298, Richmond, TW9 1BR